"Tell Me," Rosemary Demanded.

"Name some stars for me, Willis."

"Okay," he replied. But something in his voice sounded a bit strained. "Like...like Beta Pictoris, for example," he told her. "Or...or Regulus. Aldebaran. Arcturus."

The heat inside Rosemary began to churn as he rattled off the unfamiliar words, until it swirled into a seething mass of turmoil, spilling into her heart, her hands, her head. And suddenly she remembered something. She remembered that she had always been completely turned on—yes, by Willis Random, whenever he started talking like a scientist.

Because even at fifteen she had always been utterly aroused by boys who could talk intellectual talk. Mathematical talk. Scientific talk. Boys who could split atoms in their basements after dinner. And there had been only one boy at Endicott Central who could do all that.

Willis Random.

Dear Reader,

Where do you read Silhouette Desire? Sitting in your favorite chair? How about standing in line at the market or swinging in the sunporch hammock? Or do you hold out the entire day, waiting for all your distractions to dissolve around you, only to open a Desire novel once you're in a relaxing bath or resting against your softest pillow...? Wherever you indulge in Silhouette Desire, we know you do so with anticipation, and that's why we bring you the absolute best in romance fiction.

This month, look forward to talented Jennifer Greene's *A Baby in His In-Box,* where a sexy tutor gives March's MAN OF THE MONTH private lessons on sudden fatherhood. And in the second adorable tale of Elizabeth Bevarly's BLAME IT ON BOB series, *Beauty and the Brain,* a lady discovers she's still starry-eyed over her secret high school crush. Next, Susan Crosby takes readers on The Great Wife Search in *Bride Candidate #9.*

And don't miss a single kiss delivered by these delectable men: a roguish rancher in Amy J. Fetzer's *The Unlikely Bodyguard;* the strong, silent corporate hunk in the latest book in the RIGHT BRIDE, WRONG GROOM series, *Switched at the Altar,* by Metsy Hingle; and Eileen Wilks's mouthwatering honorable Texas hero in *Just a Little Bit Pregnant.*

So, no matter *where* you read, I know *what* you'll be reading— all six of March's irresistible Silhouette Desire love stories!

Regards,

Melissa Senate

Melissa Senate
Senior Editor
Silhouette Desire

Please address questions and book requests to:
Silhouette Reader Service
U.S.: 3010 Walden Ave., P.O. Box 1325, Buffalo, NY 14269
Canadian: P.O. Box 609, Fort Erie, Ont. L2A 5X3

ELIZABETH
BEVARLY
BEAUTY AND THE BRAIN

SILHOUETTE *Desire*®

Published by Silhouette Books

America's Publisher of Contemporary Romance

SILHOUETTE BOOKS

ISBN 0-373-76130-9

BEAUTY AND THE BRAIN

Books by Elizabeth Bevarly

*From Here to Maternity
†From Here to Paternity
‡The Family McCormick
**Blame It on Bob

ELIZABETH BEVARLY

is an honors graduate of the University of Louisville and achieved her dream of writing full-time before she even turned thirty! At heart, she is also an avid voyager who once helped navigate a friend's thirty-five-foot sailboat across the Bermuda Triangle. "I really love to travel," says this self-avowed beach bum. "To me, it's the best education a person can give to herself." Her dream is to one day have her own sailboat, a beautifully renovated older model forty-two footer, and to enjoy the freedom and tranquillity seafaring can bring. Elizabeth likes to think she has a lot in common with the characters she creates, people who know love and life go hand in hand. And she's getting some firsthand experience with motherhood, as well—she and her husband have a three-year-old son.

For Laurie, Debbie,
Gina and Tina,
my best buds at
Seneca High School.

Thanks for the memories.

Prologue

"**I** hate him. I despise him. I'm going to kill him."

Fifteen-year-old Rosemary March glared at the auburn-haired, bespectacled, orthodontically decorated boy on the other side of the school gymnasium and frowned.

"That pizza-faced little twerp," she said, continuing with her verbal assault. "Just who does he think he is?"

"Calm down, Rosemary," Kirby Connaught, one of her best friends, told her. "By now, nothing Willis Random does or says to you should surprise you. You guys have been mortal enemies since school started."

"Yeah," her other friend, Angie Ellison, agreed. "Just because he called you a 'simpleminded, slack-brained know-nothing' in chemistry class today. I mean, he's called you lots worse things before."

Rosemary turned her venomous gaze toward her friend in silent warning not to remind her. Angie immediately fell quiet and returned her attention to the delicate gardenia corsage that hugged her wrist.

"Yeah," Kirby concurred after a noisy slurp of her diet

soda that sucked the beverage dry. "You ought to be used to it by now. And he's going to be your lab partner for the rest of the year, so you also better get used to just ignoring him."

"Oh, thanks a lot, you two," Rosemary grumbled. "You're no help at all. I only wish I *could* ignore him. But he makes my life miserable. Not a day goes by that he doesn't make me feel like…like…"

"Like a simpleminded, slack-brained know-nothing?" Angie supplied helpfully.

Rosemary frowned harder. Yeah, she thought. Exactly like that.

The three friends were taking a break from the dancing couples who crowded the floor of the high school gymnasium. The Welcome Back Bob Comet Festival was in full swing, and the gym doors had been thrown open wide to invite in the general public and the balmy September night for the traditional Comet Stomp Dance. Rosemary's and Angie's dates had gone in search of refreshment and left the three girls to talk among themselves on the bleachers. Kirby's date…well, Kirby's date was sort of nonexistent, Rosemary knew, which was all the more reason for her to remain with her friends.

The Welcome Back Bob Comet Festival was an event that occurred in the small southern Indiana town of Endicott every decade and a half, and, as always, the community had turned out in numbers to celebrate. Comet Bob had actually made his peak appearance in the skies over town the night before, but he would be visible to the naked eye for another few days, and within telescope range for another two weeks. The Comet Festival generally ran for the entirety of Bob's appearance, for the most part constituting the whole month of September.

The festival belonged to Endicott and took place with such regularity because, for whatever reason, the comet returned to the planet like clockwork during the third week of every fifteenth September. And when it did, it always—*always*—made its closest pass at the coordinates that were exactly—*exactly*—directly above Endicott.

Bob's punctuality and preference for such specific coordinates had frustrated the studies of many a scientist since the comet's discovery nearly two centuries ago. Every fifteen years, scores of experts in the fields of astronomy, astrophysics and cosmology—and hundreds of amateurs, too—descended on southern Indiana in an effort to explain the unexplainable. And every fifteen years, those experts returned home again with notebooks full of data that defied analysis, and prescriptions for migraines that simply would not go away.

And because no one had been able to explain exactly what caused Bob's constancy or his affection for Endicott, the comet's celebrity had grown and grown, and the residents of the little Indiana town had come to claim the comet as their own.

Comet Bob actually had a much more formal name, but virtually no one could pronounce it correctly—no one but Willis Random, Rosemary thought to herself with much irritation. Because Bob was named after an eastern European scientist who had few vowels, and even fewer recognizable consonants, in his name, and who had been dead for more than a hundred years anyway, the general consensus seemed to be, *What difference does it make?*

Comet Bob was Comet Bob, and in addition to his mystery and celebrity—or perhaps, more accurately, because of it—myth and legend had grown up around his regular visits over the years. Anyone in Endicott who'd been around for more than one appearance of Bob knew full well that he was responsible for creating all kinds of mischief.

Virtually everyone was of the opinion that Bob was responsible for cosmic disturbances that caused the local citizens to behave very strangely whenever he came around. Waitresses confused restaurant orders. People got lost on their way to jobs they had been performing for years. Children cleaned their rooms and finished their homework in a timely fashion. And people who would normally never give each other the time of day fell utterly and irrevocably in love.

And, of course, there were the wishes.

It was widely believed by the townsfolk of Endicott that natives born in the small town in a year of the comet's appearance were blessed in a way no one else was. Simply put, if someone was born in the year of the comet, and if that someone made a wish the year Bob returned, while the comet was making its pass directly overhead, then that someone's wish would come true the next time Bob paid a visit.

Rosemary, Kirby and Angie had all been born the last time Bob came around. And the night before the dance, as the three girls had lain in Angie's backyard while the comet passed directly overhead, each of them had made a wish.

Angie had wished that just once, something or someone exciting would happen to the small southern Indiana town. Which, of course, Rosemary was certain now, blew any chance for the myth of the wishes to come true, because *nothing* exciting *ever* happened in Endicott.

Kirby had wished for a forever-after kind of love, the kind normally found only in books and movies. Another longshot, as far as Rosemary was concerned. Not only did Rosemary not believe in that kind of love, but Kirby hadn't ever even been on a date, let alone had anything even remotely resembling a boyfriend. All she did was go to school and take care of her invalid mother. All the boys in Endicott just thought Kirby was too *sweet* and too *nice* for any of them to ever want to take her out for romantic reasons. Not that Kirby hadn't tried.

And Rosemary... She sighed with much satisfaction now when she recalled her own wish. Rosemary had wished that that pizza-faced little twerp Willis Random would get what was coming to him someday. And *that,* she thought, was a wish with some potential. Even if she had to be the one administering justice herself, she'd see to it that somehow, some way, someday, Willis would get his.

Oh, yeah, Rosemary thought smugly as she noted again the pizza-faced little twerp standing in the corner of the gym all by himself. Someday—say fifteen years from now—Willis Random was going to pay for the way he had treated her in high school. He'd get his. She knew he would.

After all, she had Bob on her side.

One

He had been hoping Rosemary March would age badly. Even though he knew she was only thirty now, he had been praying that when he saw her again, she would be gray-haired, haggard-looking, stoop-shouldered, wrinkled and flabby. She was, after all, two years older than he was. Unfortunately, from the looks of her, Rosemary had only improved with age.

When Willis Random had rounded her kitchen doorway only seconds before and seen her for the first time in thirteen years, he had halted in his tracks, unable to say a word because his mouth and throat had suddenly gone dry. Common courtesy dictated that he should say something to make her aware of his presence in her home. Their past history together demanded that he feel defensive about it, even though he was here at her mother's invitation. But once he got a load of Rosemary standing there, he simply could not utter a sound.

Bent at the waist, she leaned lazily forward with her elbows propped on the kitchen counter. Her gaze was fixed on the dark liquid dripping methodically from the coffeemaker, her heavy-lidded eyes indicating she was clearly still half-asleep.

As if that hadn't been enough, Willis noted further with a gasp that got stuck somewhere in his throat, her attire—what little there was of it—upheld her not-quite-awake status.

Flowered cotton bikini panties hugged extremely well-rounded hips, and a cropped white undershirt revealed an expanse of creamy skin most men saw only in glossy centerfolds. She was wearing white kneesocks, too, one having fallen halfway down her calf, the other scrunched down around her ankle. Her hair was a tousle of dark brown, chin-length curls, rumpled from sleep and the fact that she had a fistful bunched in one hand.

She was a vision straight out of a thirteen-year-old boy's fantasies. And Willis should know. He'd fantasized about Rosemary March a lot when he was thirteen years old. Unfortunately, he'd never been more to her than a pizza-faced little twerp.

She must have somehow sensed his presence, because she glanced idly over at the kitchen doorway, then back at the coffeemaker again. A quick double take brought her attention back to him, and only then did Willis fully appreciate their situation.

He hadn't anticipated that their first reunion since high school graduation would play out quite like this. She was in her underwear, after all, and he was fully dressed in khaki shorts, a navy blue polo and heavy hiking boots. And although his experience with women wasn't extensive, Willis felt it was probably pretty safe to assume that most women didn't take kindly to being caught by surprise in their underthings. Particularly when the catch*er* wasn't reduced to his own Skivvies, and especially when the catcher was someone the woman had despised for more than a decade.

His suspicions were fairly well reinforced when Rosemary straightened and opened her mouth wide to emit a blood-chilling scream at the top of her lungs. He waited until she was finished, until she was staring at him silently with wide, terrified eyes, then he cleared his throat indelicately.

"Hi," he said, pretending he noticed neither her state of dishabille nor her state of distress. "I don't know if you remember me." He stuck out his hand in as matter-of-fact a gesture as he could manage and added, "I'm Willis Random. We used to go to school together."

In response to his reintroduction, Rosemary opened her mouth wide again and let out another, even more piercing, screech of horror.

Willis forced a nervous smile and dropped his hand back to his side. "Ah. I see you *do* remember me. And I'm flattered, Rosemary. Truly...flattered."

The second scream brought around Willis's companion— the mayor of Endicott, Indiana, who also happened to be Rosemary's mother—and Mrs. March joined him at the kitchen doorway.

"Rosemary, for God's sake," her mother said. "Try to be a bit more polite. I know you and Willis never got along in high school, but the least you could do is try to start off on the right foot." Mrs. March noted her daughter's attire then and made a soft *tsking* noise. "And do put some clothes on, darling. You have a guest in your house."

Then Mrs. March spun around with a quick "This way, Willis—I'll show you your room," and Willis and Rosemary were left alone again.

He scrunched up his shoulders awkwardly, then let them fall. "Good to see you again, Rosemary." As he spun around, he couldn't resist throwing over his shoulder, "All of you."

He hurried to catch up with Mrs. March before Rosemary had a chance to respond with a hastily hurled pot of coffee. A wild rush of heat that he hadn't felt in thirteen years sped through his body, but he recognized all too well. It was the feeling that had always assaulted him whenever he'd had to go toe-to-toe with Rosemary. And that had happened nearly every day when he was in the tenth grade.

The two of them had been lab partners in chemistry for an entire school year. Nine months of hell, Willis recalled now. And, he had to concede, stifling a wistful sigh that threatened, nine months of heaven, too.

He'd been the brainy geek who was skipped a couple of grades, two years younger and six inches shorter than every other guy in his class. Come to think of it, he'd also been shorter than Rosemary, and she'd doubtless outweighed him then. He'd been the proverbial ninety-seven-pound weakling until he'd taken up weight lifting in college. Of course, that second puberty he'd gone through toward the end of his sixteenth year had probably helped a lot, too.

And now he was back in Endicott, armed with five degrees—two of them doctorates—an assignment from MIT, where he currently taught astrophysics, and a high-powered telescope of his own design. He'd come back for the Comet Festival for which his hometown was famous, back for the answers that Bobrzynyckolonycki had refused to give him fifteen years before.

This time, when Willis studied the comet, he would do so with far greater knowledge and insight than he'd had when he was thirteen, the last time Bobrzynyckolonycki had come around. This time, when he collected and analyzed all of his data, it would be with infinitely more patience and attention than a teenage boy had been able to manage. This time, Willis promised himself, he was going to get the truth out of that damned comet, or he was going to die trying.

Thinking back on the vision of Rosemary and her scantily covered flesh, he bit back a groan. He'd always figured *she* would be the death of him someday. But he'd always assumed it would be her scathing words and utter contempt for him that finally did him in, and not his undying carnal desire for her. All of a sudden, he felt as if he was thirteen years old again.

And that was the last thing Willis needed. Rosemary March had made his life miserable when he was in high school. Alternately he'd hated and adored her, one minute wanting to cut her to the quick, the next minute wanting to cop a feel. She'd tied his pubescent libido in knots, something he'd never been able to understand.

Simply put, Rosemary had been an idiot, completely incapable of understanding even the most elementary scientific equation. How on earth he could have lusted after a girl who knew nothing about science, Willis had never been able to figure out. Oh, sure, she'd had a pretty face and a great body and all that, but she'd had no brain at all. How could he ever have been attracted to her? Even at thirteen, he should have been above that.

The sight of her standing half-undressed with her socks falling down around her ankles erupted in his brain again, and Willis felt himself jumping to life with a lack of control reminiscent of a thirteen-year-old boy. He clamped his teeth together tight and willed his body and libido to behave themselves. Evidently, he was still susceptible to pretty faces and great bodies, regardless of the brains that topped them.

Dammit.

Bobrzynyckolonycki, he reminded himself. *The only heavenly body you're here to study is the comet. Don't forget that.*

"Willis?" he heard Mrs. March call out some ways ahead of him. "Are you there?"

"I'm here, Mrs. March," he called back, hurrying his step to catch up with her.

And Rosemary or no Rosemary, I'm not going home until I have the answers I demand.

Rosemary March stood open-mouthed and dumbfounded in her kitchen and tried to tell herself that what she had just seen was *not* Willis Random, but an hallucination brought on by yet another late night in front of the TV, with no other companion than *The Zombies of Mora Tau* and a pint of double-chocolate-chunk fudge ice cream.

There was no way she'd believe that the big hunk of manhood lounging in her kitchen doorway moments ago—however startling his appearance had been—could have begun his life as that pizza-faced little twerp who had made Rosemary's life miserable when she was a teenager. Uh-uh. No way. No how.

The last time she'd seen Willis, he'd been giving his valedictorian speech at graduation. The class had congregated on the football field on an especially moody spring day, and Willis had literally been blown over by a good, stiff wind. Right off the podium, in front of the entire class of '85, most of whom had hooted with laughter as a result.

The man who had just left her kitchen, on the other hand…

Rosemary shook her head hard in an effort to clear it. Okay, the guy's glasses coincided with Willis's myopia, but instead of the Scotch-taped earpiece that had marked the spectacles Willis wore, this guy's were Ralph Lauren chic. And okay, the blue eyes behind the glasses were the same midnight blue that Willis's had been. She'd always marveled that such a geek should have such gorgeous eyes. And yes, the man's deep brown hair had been kissed with reddish gold highlights reminiscent of the auburn, unruly thatch that Willis had never quite been able to tame.

Other than that, there was nothing about the man who had just called himself Willis Random that even remotely resembled the obnoxious little jerk she remembered.

There was only one way to proceed with this thing, she told herself. She was going to have to follow that particular vision—and the other specter that had borne an uncanny resemblance to her own mother—and demand to know just what the hell was going on.

After she got dressed, she amended, glancing down at her attire. And after she'd poured herself a cup of coffee, she added, hearing the coffeemaker wheeze out a last gasp.

Armed with an oversize mug full of black coffee, Rosemary peeked out the kitchen doorway in an effort to discover which way her assailants had gone. Hearing nothing, she took a few silent steps toward the living room, and paused at the staircase. Muffled voices told her that her two visitors were upstairs, but she couldn't tell which room. So she padded quickly up the hardwood steps, her movements silent thanks to her stocking feet.

When she rounded the stairway landing, she saw that the attic door at the top of the staircase was agape, its collapsible steps extended down to the hallway floor. Her mother's voice carried through the opening, and Rosemary heard her saying something about the spectacular view.

Hastily, Rosemary ducked into her bedroom and closed the door behind herself. For a moment, all she could do was lean against it, trying to steady her breathing and figure out why her mother was here with a man who claimed to be Willis. True, her mother technically still owned the house that Rosemary called home, even if Janet March wasn't living here. But Rosemary had come to think of the rambling old English stucco as her own place, having lived there by herself for the last three years.

Originally, it had belonged to her maternal grandmother, who had left it to Rosemary's mother when she passed away. But Janet March had never expressed an interest in living in the hulking old house. Since the death of Rosemary's father five years ago, Janet had preferred to live in a condominium in downtown Endicott, explaining that the move would put her closer to her job, and at the heart of all the civic activities her position as mayor demanded she attend.

So her mother had offered use of the big stone-and-stucco to Rosemary if she paid the insurance and taxes, and Rosemary had jumped at the chance to live there. She'd always adored the place, and associated with it nothing but good times and warm feelings. At least, she had until she'd glanced up this morning to find a man claiming to be Willis Random haunting it.

The memory jolted her into action, and she went to her closet to tug her work uniform off its hangers. She set down her coffee long enough to throw on her straight, navy blue skirt and crisp white blouse, embroidered discreetly above the pocket *Jet-Set Travels*. She was still buttoning up the latter when she ducked out her bedroom door and into the hallway and ran right into Willis Random.

Or rather, into Willis Random's chest. Then again, seeing as how his chest had grown to roughly the size of Montana since she'd last seen him, it was kind of hard for her to miss it.

"Whoa," he said as he reached out an arm to steady her. "Where's the fire?"

She glanced up to find herself staring into midnight-blue eyes she remembered way too well for her own good, and she immediately identified the source of the fire he asked about. It was where it had always been whenever she'd had to deal with Willis, and she didn't like the realization of that now any better than she had fifteen years ago.

Oh, God, it really was Willis, she thought. He was back. And he was *beautiful*.

"Oh, God," she muttered aloud this time.

"Rosemary, please," her mother said. "Be nice to Willis. He's going to be a guest in your house for the next few weeks."

It took a moment for that to sink in, a moment Rosemary spent drinking in the sight of the man who had been her high school nemesis. The last time she'd seen Willis, he'd still stood eye-to-eye with her, in spite of his having shot up some in their junior year. His face had been a road map of state capitals, and he'd always reeked of Clearasil and Lavoris. But this Willis was so…so…so…

Wow.

He was huge. Huge. A good four inches taller than her own five-eight, and broad enough to block the sunlight streaming into the hallway from the door across the way. His skin was flawless now, deeply tanned and creased with sun-etched lines around his eyes and mouth. And what a mouth. She'd never noticed before just what beautifully formed features Willis had. And instead of Clearasil and Lavoris, he smelled of the great outdoors. Like pine trees and thunderstorms and life.

"Willis?" she finally said, her voice emerging as little more than a squeak.

"I'm baaaaack," he sang out with a smile that was completely lacking in humor. "Didja miss me?"

Even the sound of him was different, she thought, feeling as if she were descending into some kind of weird trance. His voice had deepened and grown rough over the years, just as everything else about him had seemed to do. For a moment, Rosemary could do nothing but stare at him. She simply could not believe he was the same boy who had tormented her so throughout high school. Although the potential for torment was still there, she knew without question that, these days, it would be of a decidedly less adolescent nature.

"Rosemary?" he asked. "Are you okay?"

She nodded. "Uh-huh." But she couldn't think of a single other thing to say.

Willis twisted his lips into an expression she recognized all too well. "I see you still have that vast, scintillating vocabulary I remember so well," he muttered sarcastically.

That brought her up short, and she frowned back at him. So the first shot had been fired, had it? That meant war. Willis might have changed completely on the outside, but inside, he was still the same vicious little cretin who was always putting her down and trying—usually with success—to make her feel like a fool.

Rosemary straightened, pushing herself back until she was more than an arm's length away from him. "And I see you're still Mr. Know-It-All," she countered.

She groaned inwardly. Was that the best she could do for a put-down? Dammit, Willis had always made her feel like an empty-headed, unimportant, inconsequential little gnat. Somehow, her mind had always ceased functioning whenever he was around, and not only could she never think of anything even moderately interesting to say, but she could never come up with a good comeback to his numerous assaults on her intelligence. It had just reinforced his argument that she was, quite simply, really, really stupid.

And now, here Willis stood, in her own home no less, making her feel really, really stupid all over again. It was almost more than she could bear.

"What are you doing here?" she demanded. Instead of waiting for an answer, she turned to her mother. "Mom, what's he doing here?"

Her mother smiled that soothing, complacent smile that had always made Rosemary feel anything but soothed or complacent.

"Willis is here for the Comet Festival, darling."

"I'm here to study Bobrzynyckolonycki," he announced shortly at the same time.

Rosemary blinked at the eight-syllable word that rolled so effortlessly off his tongue. "You're here to study what?" she asked. "Bobra...Bobriz..." She gave up and asked, instead, "Is that something in the water we should know about?"

Willis frowned at her again. She remembered now that he had always frowned at her, and that she'd actually wondered a time or two what he would look like if he had smiled just once, even with the sunlight glinting off his braces.

"Bob," he clarified through gritted teeth, as if he couldn't stand the sound of the word. "Bobrzynyckolonycki is 'Bob' to members of the laity, like you."

She narrowed her eyes at him. She wasn't sure what he meant by "laity," but his tone of voice indicated that whatever it was, it certainly wasn't anything good. Before she could question him about it, however, her mother began to speak again.

"Willis is on sabbatical, dear. MIT has sent him back here to figure out why Bob's appearances are so regular, and why he always makes his closest pass to the planet right above Endicott. Isn't that nice?"

Rosemary turned back to look at Willis. She should have expected something like this. He'd always been fascinated by that damned comet.

"MIT?" she echoed.

"Massachusetts Institute of Technology," he clarified.

She frowned at him. "I *know* what MIT stands for," she told him.

He arched his brows in surprise.

"I just want to know why you're here, exactly."

He nodded. "It's really very simple, Rosemary. I've designed a telescope that will enable me to gauge Bobrzynyckolonycki's approach to the earth—and, consequently, Endicott—in a rather, shall we say, unorthodox manner. That part—" he added in an offhand tone of voice "—is really much too difficult for someone like you to understand, so I won't waste my time trying to explain it. Suffice it to say that my study might potentially provide the answers to a number of questions that have puzzled the scientific community for decades."

Rosemary was too busy steaming at his easy dismissal of

her intelligence to respond to his oration. Which was just as well, because evidently, there was a lot more her mother wanted to add.

"Willis has *five* degrees," Janet gushed. "Isn't that amazing? *Five,* Rosemary. In physics, mathematics, astronomy…" Her voice trailed off and she turned to Willis for help. "What are your other two in, dear?"

"Astrophysical engineering and accounting," he told her.

Rosemary narrowed her eyes at him again. "Accounting?" she asked, finding that one a trifle out of place.

He smiled, blushing a bit. "For two wild and crazy semesters, I went a little off the deep end and thought about becoming an accountant," he told her.

She nodded, but refrained from comment.

"There, uh…" he added little sheepishly. "There was a girl involved."

Rosemary smiled inwardly. His announcement gave her the perfect opportunity to give as good as she was getting. "A girl?" she repeated, punctuating the question with what she hoped was a look of stunned disbelief. "*You* were actually *involved* with a girl? Don't tell me—let me guess. She was an exchange student who couldn't speak a word of English, from some unreachable little village in the Upper Volta where the average age of the local bachelors was seventy-two."

Willis eyed her venomously. "Oh, listen to you. You wouldn't know the Upper Volta from Butternut, Wisconsin."

Rosemary eyed him back, just as malignantly. "Oh, wouldn't I?"

Before the argument could escalate, Janet March cut in again. "And here *you* dropped out of the community college *and* beauty school, Rosemary." She punctuated her disappointment with a cluck of regret.

Rosemary bit her lip and dropped her gaze to the floor. More like she'd *flunked* out of the community college, she recalled. But she'd never tell her mother that, let alone Willis. And beauty school just hadn't been her thing—there had been too much chemistry involved. Besides, she loved her job as a travel agent. What was the big deal about college anyway?

When she looked up again, Willis was smirking at her. Actually smirking. That pizza-faced little...

Okay, so he was just a twerp now, she amended. His smirk told her that he knew exactly what was going through her head with her little self-evaluation of her failures. It also told her that he agreed more with her mother's less-than-satisfactory assessment of her.

Rosemary swallowed with some difficulty, reminded herself that she was a thirty-year-old woman with a good job and a full life, and that nobody, not her mother, not even Willis Random, was going to make her feel the way she'd always felt about herself when she was a teenager.

Self-esteem was an insidious thing, very difficult to hold on to. It had taken Rosemary years to build hers up once she'd graduated from high school, and she wasn't going to let Willis, with his five degrees and his own state-of-the-art engineering feat, tear her down again. She just wasn't.

"I have a good job, Mom," she reminded her mother in as level a voice as she could manage.

"You could have been a computer programmer," her mother reminded her back, "if you'd stayed enrolled at the community college."

Willis barked out a laugh at that. "You?" he asked Rosemary incredulously. "*You* were studying computer programming? You're joking, right? You couldn't possibly fathom anything as mentally challenging as that."

Mrs. March sighed again, this time with even more disappointment. "Yes, I suppose her father and I should have realized when Rosemary started that it wasn't really the thing for her. But she seemed so intent on it at the time. It was almost as if she were trying to prove something. I just didn't have the heart to try to talk her out of it."

Something cold and wet landed hard in the pit of Rosemary's stomach, but she turned to face Willis fully. "Yeah, me," she said. "I studied computer programming for a whole semester. Then I realized that you were right about me, Willis. I wasn't cut out for college. And I certainly wasn't cut out for science. So I found a job I like just fine. And I'm good at it, too, okay?''

He was silent for a moment, and she wished more than anything in the world that she could understand what that intense expression on his face meant. "So what do you do for a living these days?'' he finally asked her.

She almost believed he cared. Almost. "I'm a travel agent," she replied, telling herself there was no reason for her to feel so defensive.

He nodded. "Then I guess you finally get to visit all those places you used to talk about visiting, hmm?''

Her mother waved her hand airily and smiled. "Oh, Rosemary never goes anywhere, do you, darling? She has a terrible fear of flying, not to mention claustrophobia, and she suffers from violent motion sickness.''

Willis threw Rosemary another odd look at that, but she couldn't for the life of her figure out what it meant. Instead she cursed him for coming back to Endicott, and wondered at her mother's assertion that he would be a guest in her house.

"Why are you here?'' she asked again.

"I told you, dear,'' her mother interjected. "He's studying the comet.''

Rosemary turned to face her mother. "No, I mean, what's he doing *here*—in my house?''

Janet March smiled that unsettling smile again. "He's going to be staying here at the house with you during Bob's visit.''

Rosemary's eyebrows shot up at that. "I beg your pardon?''

Her mother opened her mouth to reply, but Willis raised a hand to stop her. "Allow me, Mrs. March.''

He looked down at Rosemary, silently for a moment, as if he were trying to figure out just how to say what he had to say so that an imbecile would understand it. She felt her back go up. Fast.

"Your house is situated perfectly for me to view Bobrzynyckolonycki,'' he said. "The trajectory—'' He stopped, as if he feared any word with more than two syllables might be too big a challenge for her.

"I know what a trajectory is,'' she told him crisply.

He seemed genuinely surprised. "Do you?"

She nodded, but suddenly felt less certain. "I think."

"Well, let me just put it this way," he began again. "Your house is situated perfectly for me to observe both the comet's approach *and* its departure."

"Why my house?"

"It's well outside the city limits and up here on a hill all by itself. There are no lights from downtown Endicott to interfere with my viewing of the night sky. And the chemical reaction from traffic and industry is minimal—thus they won't interfere with atmospheric conditions. And it's quiet and secluded, which will be enormously helpful while I'm collecting and analyzing my data. Best of all, your attic windows are almost perfectly aligned with the comet's path—all we'll have to do is take out the slats. And with your attic being the massive size that it is, I can set up my telescope with little difficulty."

"You see?" her mother concluded with a smile, taking each of Rosemary's hands affectionately in her own. "This is the perfect place for Willis to perform his work. So he'll be staying here in the house with you for the duration of his study."

Rosemary looked first at Willis, then at her mother, then back at Willis. "The hell he will," she said.

Her mother frowned at her. "Rosemary, don't you *dare* swear in my presence."

She felt immediately and properly chastened, and blushed deeply. "I'm sorry, Mom." However, she quickly recovered enough to add, "But he can't stay here."

"Of course he can."

"No, he can't."

"Why not?"

"Because I don't want him to."

Janet March's smile returned, and it grated on Rosemary even more than usual. "Darling, that's perfectly understandable," her mother cooed, "given the history the two of you share." She dropped one of her daughter's hands and curled her fingers around Willis's solid arm to include him in the discussion. "But you're both adults now, and I know you're above all that adolescent bickering you used to engage in."

"But, Mom—" Rosemary began.

Janet turned to her and interrupted, "And, Rosemary, darling, not only is Willis working on a very important study for the scientific community, what he's doing will add beautifully to the festival."

"But, Mom—"

"Imagine the media coverage. It will be good PR. And you know how important that is to Endicott."

"But, Mom—"

"The revenue generated during the Comet Festival is what keeps this town afloat. And I don't have to remind you that we only have the opportunity to take advantage of it every fifteen years."

"But, Mom—"

"And besides, darling, this is still *my* house."

Well, that certainly shut Rosemary up. Her mother had never invoked ownership privilege for anything before.

"And speaking as both mayor and citizen of Endicott, I'm inviting Willis to be a guest in my house for as long as he needs to be." She fixed her gaze intently on her daughter. "Will that be a problem, Rosemary?"

Rosemary returned her mother's gaze, feeling a heavy weight descend upon her shoulders. Her mother was right— the house belonged to her. She could invite whomever she pleased to be a guest, and there wouldn't be a whole lot Rosemary could do about it. Still, it would have been nice if, just once, her mother had taken her daughter's feelings into consideration over what might be best for the community.

But Janet March was a much better mayor than she had ever been a mother. It's why she'd spent three consecutive terms in office and would doubtless be elected to another.

It wasn't bitterness on Rosemary's part that caused her to draw such a conclusion. It was simply a fact of her life that her mother had never taken as much interest in the wants and needs of her children as she had her own civic activities. Oh, Janet had been a nice enough mother, and even considerate in her own, rather shortsighted way. But she'd never been particularly good at mothering. And, if pressed, even Janet herself would probably laugh and admit that such a thing was true.

Rosemary knew there was no way her mother would bend on the idea of having Willis stay right here in the big English stucco with her. Short of moving out herself, Rosemary was stuck with him as a house guest for the next few weeks, if that was what Mayor Janet March decreed. And there was no way Rosemary would be moving out. Even if she could have afforded to rent something else for that length of time, thanks to the Comet Festival, there wasn't a room available within a hundred miles of Endicott.

And even though Angie and Kirby would probably open their homes to her, Rosemary couldn't find it in herself to impose on her friends for that length of time. Angie's apartment was barely big enough for one. And besides, Angie was way too busy investigating the appearance in town of that lowlife, scumbag, murdering slug Ethan Zorn to want Rosemary bothering her.

And although Kirby had an extra bedroom at her house, Rosemary didn't want to crimp her friend's style trying to snag a man. Even though there was little chance that Kirby, the Endicott equivalent to Mother Teresa, was *ever* going to land herself a local boy, because all the local boys just thought Kirby was far too sweet and far too nice to ever try something like…like…like *that* with her. Not that Kirby hadn't tried.

It was a big house, Rosemary told herself. With any luck at all, she and Willis wouldn't even have to see each other during his stay. With any luck at all, he'd banish himself to the attic with his notebook and his telescope and his scientific equations, which he found infinitely more interesting than he found her anyway. With any luck at all, he'd leave her alone and keep to himself.

And with any luck at all, she thought further with a helpless sigh, she wouldn't find herself feeling like the know-nothing jerk she'd always been convinced she was whenever she was around Willis.

"Fine," she capitulated reluctantly. Swallowing a groan,

she turned to her old nemesis and added halfheartedly, "Welcome home, Willis. It hasn't been the same around here without you."

And with that, she spun around and made her way back downstairs, completely uncaring that her coffee still sat untouched in her bedroom. It was just her first indication that things were only going to get worse.

Two

What had she meant by that? Willis wondered. Why had Rosemary said Endicott hadn't been the same without him? Was that good? Or was that bad? Surely it must be the former. She'd always hated his guts. Or was she just trying to confuse him, trying to tie him up in knots again, the way she always had when they'd been in school?

God, he hated having to do this. If it wasn't for the fact that his need to explain the comings and goings of Bobrzynckolonycki far outweighed any lingering ill will he harbored toward Rosemary March, he'd pick up his bags and his telescope and head back to Cambridge in a heartbeat. But he knew he wouldn't do that, because the comet had haunted him for fifteen years.

Of course, so had Rosemary March, he reminded himself. But for entirely different reasons. Where Willis had never been able to pinpoint the comet's motivation for its activities, he'd more than understood Rosemary's. She had despised him—that was all there was to it. Doubtless she despised him still. Then again, he supposed he had no one but himself to blame for that. He hadn't exactly made it easy on her all those years ago.

And he wasn't making it easy on her now, either, he thought, an odd kind of guilt nagging at him. Why had he had to go and shoot his mouth off about her being too stupid to understand something like computer programming? That had been uncalled for, even if it was true. He'd just been smarting from her suggestion that no woman in her right mind would ever take an interest in him, and he'd struck back without thinking.

It was going to be a long few weeks.

He turned to Rosemary's mother and forced a smile. "Thanks again, Mrs. March, for putting me up this way," he said. "Especially on such short notice."

She returned his smile. "You should really be thanking Rosemary, not me. Even though this *is* my house, I hate pulling rank on her like this. Still, it's for the good of the community, isn't it?"

"It's for the good of the world," Willis corrected her. "If I can ultimately decipher a reason for why Bobrzynyckolonycki's movements through the cosmos are what they are, this year's festival will go down in history."

And, of course, he thought further with a satisfied smile, so would he. And that ought to show Rosemary March once and for all that he was a lot more than the pizza-faced little twerp she'd always considered him to be.

God, where had that come from? he wondered. What did he care what Rosemary thought of him? Her opinion of him today mattered about as much to him now as it had when he was thirteen years old. So there.

He followed Mrs. March back outside, then bade her goodbye beside his Montero—loaded to the gills with all of his paraphernalia—that he'd parked on the street in front of the house. The parts for his telescope would be arriving the following day, so he had twenty-four hours to unpack, get settled and reacquaint himself with his surroundings. Twenty-four hours to prowl Endicott and remember what his life as a boy had been like all those years ago.

Because his parents had moved to Florida after he graduated from high school and his sister had headed west, Willis hadn't had any reason to come back to the community where he'd grown up. When he'd left Endicott for MIT thirteen years ago, he'd known he would be returning for the Comet Festival this year. But he'd had no idea he would have such mixed feelings about his return. He had never been particularly fond of his hometown, or of many of its residents. Thanks to his brilliant mind and geek status, he'd just never felt as if he belonged here. The town was too cozy, too comfortable, too set in its ways. And in no way conducive to scientific thought.

He was already looking forward to getting back to Boston, back to the wealth of academic and thought-provoking opportunities available there. That city was teeming with life for people like Willis—people who needed constant mental exercise and continuous cerebral challenge. He felt alive when he was in the city.

Intellectually, at least. What difference did it make if his social life had lain dormant for some time? Who needed romantic entanglements when they had a brain like his? As far as he was concerned, the heart, as an organ, was highly overrated, in spite of its necessity for sustaining life.

After all, what good was living if you couldn't experience life at its fullest? And how could you experience life at its fullest unless you had the intellectual capacity to appreciate it? Any scientist worth his NaCl would tell you that the head, not the heart, was where the greatest stimulation occurred.

Willis popped open the back door on the Montero and wondered what to unload first—boxes of books, cartons of astronomical charts or stacks of scientific data he'd been collecting for the last fifteen years. So intent was he on his decision that he didn't hear Rosemary come up behind him. What alerted him to her arrival was the light fragrance of something soft and fresh and sweet, an aroma that immediately carried him backward in time fifteen years.

Whatever Rosemary sprayed on herself now, she'd been using it for at least a decade and a half. And it wreaked all kinds of havoc with both Willis's olfactory senses and his carnal ones—just as it had when he was a teenager. In spite of the antagonism that had erupted between the two of them whenever they were close, he'd always thought Rosemary March smelled wonderful. When he spun around to face her, he found her shrugging into a navy blue blazer and eyeing him with trepidation.

"Need any help?" she asked, her voice actually civil.

He nodded toward her attire. "You're not exactly dressed to be unloading boxes."

She straightened her collar, and again, he was assaulted by her delicate scent. "If you can wait until this afternoon, I can give you a hand with that. I'm only working a half day today."

He shook his head. "That's okay. Most of it's probably too heavy for you."

She frowned at him. "Oh, so now I'm not only stupid, but I'm weak, too—is that it?"

He closed his eyes and sighed heavily, and wondered if there would ever be a time when the two of them could converse without every word being misconstrued as an insult. "No," he told her. "That wasn't what I meant at all. These boxes are loaded with books and other instruments that are bulky and heavy. Too heavy for you." As an afterthought, he added, "Thanks anyway."

As if she needed to prove something to him, however, she pushed past him and reached for one of the boxes nearest the door. He started to reach for it, too, but something in her posture warned him off. Rosemary hefted the carton into her hands, staggered some under its weight, then moved awkwardly toward the grass.

As she bent to place it on the ground, however, she began to teeter forward. And Willis, recognizing the box as the one holding a number of glass lenses that were irreplaceable—at least in Endicott—quickly moved to her side to take it from her. She glared at him when he did, but he set it effortlessly on the ground.

"It's very expensive, very specialized, very scientific equipment," he told her.

Her eyes widened in obviously feigned admiration. "Ooo,

very scientific, huh? Like what? Like Magic Rocks and Sea Monkeys and stuff?''

He ignored the question. "It's equipment I wouldn't be able to replace with a simple trip down to Buck's hardware store.''

"Fine," she bit out. "Forget I offered. Jeez, Willis, I was just trying to be nice. But don't worry—I won't be stupid enough to do that again.''

She started to stalk off, and impulsively, he followed her, reaching out to snag her wrist with loosely curled fingers before he even realized what he was doing. Rosemary spun around with the force of a cyclone and jerked her hand back, cradling it in her other as if she had been burned. The look in her eyes when she met his gaze very nearly overwhelmed him, so brimming with anger and sadness was it, that Willis took a step backward in defense.

"Don't you ever do that again," she told him, backing away from him as she did.

"What?" he asked, genuinely confused. "All I did was take your hand.''

"That's exactly what I mean.''

"But—"

"Just stay away from me, Willis," she said, backing up a few more steps.

"What, you can't even stand my touch?" he snarled. He shook his head in confusion, his own anger swelling to life now. "Hey, you were the one who came up to me, not the other way around,'' he reminded her.

"Yeah, and it was a pretty dumb thing to do, too." She took another step backward, her eyes clouding even more.

"Rosemary…'' he began, taking an experimental step forward.

Why he bothered he couldn't imagine. He'd never made an effort to smooth out the feathers he ruffled on her before. But there was something in her eyes now that hadn't been there fifteen years ago when he'd challenged her. Back in high school, Rosemary had always fought him with every ounce of indignation she possessed. Now, however, it was almost as if she were giving up when the battle hadn't even begun.

And before he could say whatever it was he had intended to tell her—which, frankly, he couldn't remember now—she turned her back on him and began stalking once more toward her garage.

"I have to go to work," she announced stiffly.

As he stood there watching her mutely, she unfolded the doors on the aged garage and, in no time at all, was backing out of the driveway in a shiny red convertible that Willis found in no way surprising. That was Rosemary. All flash, no substance. Great body, but no head at all. Impulsive, spontaneous, breezy, fun-loving. Everything he wasn't. Everything he tried to avoid.

Yet everything he'd always ended up looking for in another woman, and had never been able to find.

Dammit.

Rosemary March had ruined him for other women, and he hadn't even had the opportunity to experience her. In spite of the fact that she was the last kind of female he should be attracted to, she'd been the first one he'd had a crush on, the first one he'd lusted after, however stupid it had been for him to want her.

And somehow, that had defined his taste in women for the rest of his life. Although he'd tried to establish relationships with good, solid, intelligent women—attractive women at that, and women who appreciated what he had to offer intellectually, women who likewise challenged his own IQ—he suddenly realized that he was doomed to want spirit and fluff, instead. Like Rosemary March.

As he watched the little red sports car with the gorgeous brunette at the wheel disappear around the corner with far more speed than was prudent, Willis realized something else, too. It wasn't that he was destined to spend his life wanting women *like* Rosemary March. No, he was condemned to spend his life wanting *her*. Specifically. Ironically. Erotically. Eternally.

Dammit.

A woman who had nothing to offer him beyond the physical, who would challenge him in none of the intellectual ways he wanted and needed to be challenged. A woman he could certainly be satisfied with sexually, but who would do nothing to fulfill his other, metaphysical, needs. A woman who would make his daily life hell because he would constantly be tied in knots wanting more than she could ever hope to give him.

A woman who would never even like him, let alone love him, he reminded himself. So what was he getting all worked up about anyway? It wasn't like Rosemary would ever return any overture he might make. Thanks to some of the things he'd said and done to her fifteen years ago, she would despise him for the rest of her life. Worrying about a future with her was pointless, because he didn't have a hope in hell of *having* a future with her. Not that he truly wanted one anyway.

He expelled a restless breath and scrubbed a hand viciously through his hair, then turned back to the task at hand. He had a lot of unloading to do, he reminded himself, and a lot of unpacking, too. And not just of the material things he'd brought with him on this particular journey, either. Willis was carrying around a lot more baggage than he'd realized, and he'd brought it all back home to Endicott. Yeah, he had a lot of sorting and unpacking to do while he was in town. And a good bit of it was in no way scientific.

For an intelligent man, he thought to himself, he sure did do some stupid things.

Rosemary pulled into her driveway after work and sat in her car with the motor off, staring at her front door. She was actually dreading to enter the house she'd loved all her life, fearful of what she would find inside. Visions of the new-and-improved Willis had assailed her all day while she was at work, making her lose her place and forget what she was doing. She'd done nothing but make mistakes—dumb mistakes—the whole time she was working. And she'd felt like an idiot as a result.

Because all she'd been able to do, instead, was daydream about Willis. Willis draped over her sofa with the Sunday sports page. Willis sharing a cup of coffee with her in the morning before she left for work. Willis mowing the grass in the backyard. Or changing a spark plug on her car. Or lifting a baby high above his head with a laugh. Or leaving the bathroom amid a puff of steam, wearing nothing but a loose towel wrapped around his waist.

She squeezed her eyes shut as that last scene unfolded in her brain. Boy, was she desperate. The first guy that wandered into her house, she had him nailed down for husband-and-father material.

Rosemary would have been lying if she said she didn't want to settle down with the right man. But she just hadn't *met* the right man. Most of the boys she'd gone to high school with had left town to go to college, and they'd either stayed gone or come back with wives or fiancées. And the few single newcomers who had managed to wander into Endicott just hadn't been her type. She would have loved to be married and raising kids by now, had she found someone who wanted to share such a future with her.

But this was *Willis* she was fantasizing about now, she reminded herself ruthlessly. *Willis,* for God's sake. *Willis!*

Willis who hated her guts and made her feel like an imbecile. Who dismissed her with all the consideration of a mosquito about to be squashed. Who would do nothing but make her feel like less and less of a functional human being if she was ever stupid enough to get involved with him.

Not that he had offered her any indication that he wanted any kind of involvement, she reminded herself. Oh, no. On the contrary, he'd made it clear from the get-go that he thought she was still the simpleminded, slack-brained know-nothing he'd pegged her as back in tenth grade. And considering the idiocy of her daydreams at work, she wasn't entirely sure she could disagree with him at the moment.

Of course, there could be a perfectly logical explanation for her fantasies, she reminded herself hopefully. Comet Bob was looming out there on the horizon, and everyone in Endicott knew that Bob was responsible for creating a cosmic interference that wreaked all kinds of havoc with the townsfolk, not the least of which was driving together romantically two people who were normally at polar opposites.

Yeah, that was it, she told herself. The comet might just be within range enough now to be putting everyone under its cosmic influence, herself included. It was entirely possible that Rosemary was simply succumbing to a galactic disturbance over which she had absolutely no control whatsoever. The reason she suddenly found Willis at the center of her romantic fantasies wasn't that she was honestly attracted to him, but that she'd simply been pulled into the sphere of Bob's influence.

Yeah, that was it, she thought again. Maybe she could just blame the whole thing on Bob.

Then again, maybe Bob had nothing to do with it, she thought irritably. Then again, maybe she was just developing a big ol' whopping crush on Willis Random.

She leaned forward until her forehead rested on the steering wheel, then slowly and methodically began to beat her head against it in an attempt to pound some sense into her brain. The only person on earth who genuinely despised her, and she might just have a crush on him. Surely there were twelve-step programs for women like her. Maybe she should look in the Yellow Pages.

She stopped bashing her head against the steering wheel and looked up again, only to find that Willis was standing on her front porch watching her. She closed her eyes again, wondering if he'd witnessed her attempted self-inflicted lobotomy, then decided that the way things were going, he must have. Could her life possibly get any worse?

It had to be Bob, she told herself, meeting his gaze as levelly as she could. Yeah, sure, Willis was a prime physical specimen of manhood these days, but he was still a big jerk. There was no way she would normally feel affection for such a man. No way would she fall in love with someone who would always make her feel small.

Inhaling a fortifying breath, she opened her car door and unfolded herself from the front seat, then reached back in behind herself for her blazer. The September afternoon was warm, the sun hung high in the sky and Willis was looking at her with something truly hot and smoldering in his eyes. That look, more than anything else, she decided, was what caused the perspiration that suddenly seemed to be dampening her shirt.

He was angry at her already, she thought. And she hadn't even walked in the front door yet.

"We have a problem," he said by way of a greeting as she stepped up onto the front porch.

He was just now realizing that? she wondered. Gee, she'd had that one figured out way back in tenth grade. Some genius *he* was. But aloud, she only said, "Oh? What's that?"

In response to her question, he frowned and jabbed a thumb angrily over his shoulder, toward the front door. Gingerly, Rosemary preceded him through it. Inside, she saw nothing out of the ordinary. Sunlight filtered through the lace curtains on the bay windows, scattering rampant shadows over her grandmother's hooked flowered rug and the antique furniture that was arranged exactly as it had been when Rosemary was a girl. Her cat, Ska, was curled up on the window seat in the shape of a Christmas ham, just as she always was this time of day, her silver-and-gray-and-black striped fur sleek and shiny.

"What?" Rosemary asked when she saw nothing amiss.

Willis pointed to the cat. "That."

Puzzled, she asked, "Are you allergic to cats?"

He shook his head. "No, I'm not. That's not the problem."

"Then what is?"

"She is. She's a bully."

Rosemary couldn't help the ripple of laughter that escaped her. "Ska? A bully? Don't be silly. She's the sweetest creature on the face of the earth."

"Her *name* is *Ska?*" he asked, arching one brow in disbelief.

As always, after two minutes in Willis's presence, Rosemary zoomed from defensive to combative in a nanosecond. "Yeah. Her name is Ska. You wanna make something of it?"

He shook his head. "I should have known. That was what you called that strange music you always listened to in high school."

She took a step forward and settled her hands on her hips

in challenge. "I still listen to Ska bands. All the time. They're coming back now, you know. You wanna make something of it?"

Willis, too, advanced toward her, crowding her space. "No, I just want you to tell that animal to be a little nicer."

As if realizing she was the topic of the conversation, Ska woke up and blinked her eyes at the couple, then stood and stretched. With a final flexing of her claws, she leaped down to the floor, then sauntered over to Rosemary, entwining herself around her mistress's legs with much affection. Rosemary picked her up and scratched her behind the ears, and Ska settled into a contented, rumbling purr.

"I can't believe you're afraid of a sweet little kitty-cat," she told Willis.

Willis frowned at her. "*I'm* not afraid of her. *He* is." He gestured behind himself, toward a ventilated cat carrier surrounded by some of the boxes that had come out of his big...his big...truck thing.

"Who is?" she asked.

"Isosceles."

Rosemary narrowed her eyes at him. "Excuse me?"

He expelled an impatient sigh, then strode over to the carrier in question, flipped open the door and withdrew a huge, hulking white cat that claimed a gorgeous, sleek coat of fur. "This," he told her, clutching the monstrous beast to his chest, "is Isosceles. My cat."

Now it was Rosemary's turn to go on the offensive. "What the hell kind of name is 'Isosceles' for a cat? Don't you realize that's just asking all the other cats in the neighborhood to beat him up after school every day?"

"It's a perfectly appropriate name," Willis countered. "Every time he sits down, he forms an exact isosceles triangle."

Rosemary arched her brows. "What did you do? Take out your compass and protractor and measure him yourself?"

Willis gritted his teeth. "You don't use a compass for measuring triangles," he told her. "They're for drawing accurate circles."

Rosemary felt her face flame, though whether in embarrassment or anger, she couldn't have said. "So what?" she bit out defensively.

He shook his head in annoyance. "So that...that...that bully you call a sweet little kitty-cat has been after Isosceles ever since I brought him inside the house."

"Well, duh," Rosemary said. "Of course she has. This is Ska's turf. She's not going to just sit back and let some interloper overrun the place." Unlike her gutless mistress, she thought further to herself.

"Well, just tell her to back off and give Isosceles a chance, all right?"

Rosemary gazed down at Ska, who looked back at her with a contented little smile. "Good girl," she told the cat. "Don't let that invading, know-it-all tomcat take over the ground you worked so hard to gain. Now go out there and make me proud."

With a quick kiss to the cat's muzzle, she settled her back on the floor and returned her attention to Willis. "There. That ought to take care of it," she said as Ska trotted happily toward the dining room, tail held high.

Willis glowered at her, then held Isosceles aloft, meeting the white cat's blue-eyed gaze levelly. "You do whatever you have to do to make her come around and treat you like the good guy you are," he coached the animal emphatically. "You're a guest here, not to mention smarter than the average cat. Don't let her treat you like dirt." He ruffled the cat's ears affectionately before settling him, too, on the floor, and immediately, Isosceles skittered off in the same direction as Ska.

A moment of silence descended where Rosemary and Willis eyed each other warily, both of them clearly aware that there had been a lot more to those little feline pep talks than either had let on. Then a crash, followed by the angry whining and hissing of two cats, caused them both to race toward the kitchen.

Ska had Isosceles treed on top of the refrigerator, and both animals were batting wildly at each other with claws unsheathed despite the distance that separated them.

"He just better stay away from her kibble," Rosemary muttered. "You mess with Ska's kibble, you pay. Big-time."

"Believe me," Willis countered, "he wants nothing to do with her plebeian kibble. He's on the *Science* Diet."

She rolled her eyes. "I should have guessed."

Knowing Ska would be fine on her own, Rosemary pushed herself off the kitchen doorjamb and made her way toward the stairs. More than anything, she wanted to slip out of her work uniform and into something comfortable. Then she reminded herself that as long as Willis Random was living under her roof, she wasn't likely to find comfort in much of anything.

"Rosemary," he called out just as her foot touched the bottom step.

She turned around to find him standing framed by the arch separating dining room from living room. Boy, he had great legs, she thought, letting her gaze travel from his boot-clad ankles to the muscular thighs extending from the brief khaki shorts.

"Hmmm…?" she asked distractedly.

"She won't…hurt him. Will she?"

Rosemary tried to smile with some reassurance, but she only felt oddly melancholy. "Ska wouldn't hurt anybody," she promised. "She might mess with his head a little—just to keep things level—but she won't hurt him."

Willis nodded, but still didn't seem quite convinced.

"How about Isosceles?" she asked.

He seemed stumped by the question. "What about him?"

"He won't hurt Ska, will he?"

The expression Willis gave her was incredulous. "Are you serious? Do you honestly think he has it in him to do harm to her?"

She nodded. "Yeah, I do. He's a lot bigger than she is. And you said yourself that he's smarter than the average cat."

"He may be smart, but he's not mean," Willis assured her. "He won't hurt Ska. Don't give it another thought."

She nodded, but still felt unsettled for some reason. "Will you be around for dinner?" she asked.

His expression indicated he was genuinely surprised by her

question—maybe as surprised as she was to hear herself making the offer. "I…I guess so," he replied. "I mean, if you want me to be."

"Oh, no," she countered quickly, wanting to dissuade him of *that* idea as quickly as possible. Even if it *was* true, she realized morosely. "It's not that. Just…if you're going to be here… I mean…"

Well, just what *did* she mean? she asked herself. She inhaled a deep breath and tried again. "I don't know what you and my mom worked out with meals and all, but… What I mean is… I don't usually go to a lot of trouble, but if you want to join me for dinner while you're staying here, I…I guess I won't mind."

"Thanks," he said, his expression revealing nothing of what he might actually be thinking. "I honestly hadn't thought too much about where I'd be eating. I don't know how often I'll be able to take advantage of your invitation, but I appreciate it your extending it."

"It *wasn't* an invitation," she felt it necessary to clarify, feeling both stung that he hadn't leaped on the opportunity and puzzled as to why she should care. "It just doesn't make sense for you to drive all the way into town to eat, when there's a perfectly good kitchen right here."

"Okay," he said. "It's not an invitation. I still appreciate the offer."

"It wasn't an offer, either."

He expelled an exasperated sound. "Well, whatever it was, thank you, all right?"

She nibbled her lip a little anxiously. "You're welcome. Just let me know when you'll be home."

His lips curled into something of a smile, however stiff. "I think I can probably make it tonight."

She nodded, her stomach clutching nervously for some reason. "Okay. I usually eat about six. If you're here, fine. If you're not here, that's fine, too."

"Fine."

Silence hovered between them until it began to grow awkward. Then another loud thump from the kitchen, followed by an even louder feline wail, sliced through the room. Willis bolted toward it, while Rosemary stood at the foot of the stairs in bemusement, watching him go. She didn't understand why she'd asked Willis to join her for dinner while he was staying with her. But there was one thing she did understand—too well.

It was going to be a long few weeks.

Three

At 6:30 that evening, a quickly cooling casserole was sitting on the stove, Rosemary was seated at the head of her recently dusted dining-room table, Ska was supping noisily from her bowl in the kitchen, Isosceles was still atop the refrigerator—and Willis was nowhere to be found. He'd left shortly after Rosemary had arrived home, without even telling her goodbye, and she had no idea where he was now. Obviously, someplace infinitely more important than where she was herself, she thought. But then, was that really such a surprise?

She stood and snuffed out the candles she felt foolish now for ever having retrieved from the china cabinet, and replaced them where they always sat, unused. She cleared the table of the colorful pottery dinner plates and crackled cranberry glassware she normally saved for special occasions, returning them, too, to their generally neglected kitchen cupboard. Then she swept the recently ironed tablecloth from the dining-room table and stuffed it back into the drawer where it had lain unused since the last time Rosemary had invited someone over for dinner—Kirby and Angie, four months earlier.

She sighed as she set the kitchen table—for one—with her usual plain white dishes and discount-store glassware on a plastic place mat. She wondered who she thought she'd been kidding, thinking dinner with Willis would be a special occasion. He hadn't even considered it a big enough deal to call her and tell her he wouldn't be there when he'd changed his mind.

And she'd actually *prepared* something. Something that hadn't come out of a cardboard box or a plastic bag. Something with *ingredients,* for God's sake. Ingredients she'd had to drive to the grocery store to buy, because who in her right mind actually kept things like garlic and onions and cream of mushroom soup on hand?

Well, come to think of it, probably a lot of people, she realized. People who cooked their food instead of microwaving it, people who cared about the flavor of what they ate, people who spent more than four to six minutes boiling something for dinner. People who didn't live alone.

She plopped a generous helping of the casserole messily onto her plate, slapped some greens into her salad bowl and splashed some iced tea into her glass. Except for Ska's crunching, the house was unnervingly quiet, so Rosemary switched on the radio before she sat down. Mellow jazz music filled the kitchen, and a soft breeze rattled the loosely hooked screen door. But it was still too quiet. Funny, she'd never noticed that about her house before.

She'd stashed the leftovers, washed her dishes and placed bowls of food and water on top of the refrigerator for Isosceles—leaving the Little Friskies box up there with the cat, because doubtless he liked to read the nutrition information while he was eating—when she heard the rumble of Willis's big truck thing outside. Tamping down the irritation that flared, she forced herself to remain cool and collected.

Indifferent. That's what she wanted him to think she was. That's what she wished she could actually feel. Totally and completely unaffected by his return to her life. Hey, what did she care whether or not he ate his dinner with her? What difference did it make if he had found something better to do than spend time with her? What did it matter if he thought so little of her that he hadn't even called her to let her know he wouldn't be there?

It didn't matter at all, she reminded herself. None of it mattered. She and Willis had been sworn enemies for half their lives. Had she really expected that to change just because they were older and allegedly more mature now? Just because there was some distance between the past and the present? Just because the two of them had been separated for a long time?

Hadn't they both reverted immediately to childish behavior the moment they'd encountered each other? she asked herself further. She supposed there were just some things in life that were simply too difficult to be completely overcome. And being constantly belittled and dismissed by someone for years was obviously one of them.

Rosemary knew she and Willis were equally guilty for saying and doing unkind things to each other when they were kids. But hurts like that, when one was so young, cut deep into a person's spirit, a person's soul. And she supposed it would take a bigger person than she—or Willis—was to simply put those differences aside and be friends.

Therefore, she knew she had no right to blame him for standing her up. Had the situation been reversed, had she told him she would join him for dinner and then found something—or someone—more interesting to occupy her time, then she probably would have stood him up, too.

So why was she so angry? she wondered. Why did she feel so insulted? Why, dammit, were her feelings so hurt?

The front door opened, so Rosemary didn't have time to find an answer for those questions. Instead, she put a rush order on her emotions to get ahold of themselves. Willis rounded the kitchen doorway just as she finally settled her pulse rate to a manageable level, and the huge grin that split his face immediately disappeared when he saw her.

For just the briefest of moments, while that smile had been in place, Willis had looked so handsome he'd nearly taken her breath away. She'd never seen him smile like that when they were kids—certainly not at her. Whoever he'd spent his evening with had obviously been someone special. And why on earth did it open up a big, gaping hole inside her to realize that?

She must not have been very successful in hiding her feelings, because he took one look at her face and said, "You were expecting me for dinner, weren't you?"

She shrugged, hoping the gesture looked nonchalant, when nonchalant was the last thing she felt. "Why would I be expecting you for dinner? Just because you told me you'd be here? That's no reason, is it?"

She cursed herself for the brittleness of her response, but yes, she had been expecting him. And it hurt that he hadn't even had enough consideration for her to pick up the phone and tell her he wouldn't be there, even if such a thing should come as no surprise at all.

"I didn't tell you for sure that I'd be here," he reminded her.

She shrugged again, the gesture feeling awkward enough that she knew it was in no way convincing. "Fine. You didn't tell me for sure. My mistake. I stand corrected."

"It's just that I was in town, having a look around, and I ran into Mr. Jamiolkowski, the physics teacher at Central—remember him?" Before Rosemary had a chance to respond, Willis quickly interjected, "Oh, no, of course you don't. You didn't take physics, did you? You had to be in the advanced program to enroll."

She dropped her gaze to the floor. As if she needed to be reminded of *that*. "No," she said softly. "I took senior foods, instead. I learned my lesson with chemistry not to take on more than I could handle."

"Well, anyway," Willis continued, obviously oblivious to her discomfort, "he and I became fairly close while I was a student—we even corresponded during my first two years at MIT—and it was just so good to see him again that we wound up having dinner together."

"Fine," Rosemary repeated.

"He's working on an amazing project," Willis went on, "something that's truly revolutionary. But he's only able to carry out his research during summer vacation. I don't know why he bothers to teach high school. He has so much to bring to the scientific community. It's terrible to see such a brilliant mind wasted like that.''

Rosemary snapped her head back up at Willis's dismissive tone of voice. ''You think teaching kids is a waste of time?'' she asked.

His expression was the same as it would have been if she had just asked him to swallow hemlock. ''Well, of course it is, when one is clearly more suited to scientific research.''

''Maybe Mr. Jamiolkowski feels he's more useful as a guide for young minds than he would be locked up in some think tank somewhere.''

Willis shook his head and chuckled. ''What an absurd suggestion.''

''Maybe he *likes* teaching, Willis. Maybe he thinks it's more important to contribute to the education of kids than it is to work in some sterile laboratory for his own satisfaction, or because eggheads like you think he should. Maybe *teaching* is what brings him satisfaction. Not scientific research.''

''That's ridiculous,'' Willis told her. ''Why would a brilliant man waste his time on something other than research?''

She shook her head in wonder. ''Boy, you really don't get it, do you?''

''Get what?''

She watched him in silence for a moment, then sighed. ''Never mind. For a guy with a high IQ, you really have a lot to learn.''

''Oh, and coming from you, that's an admonition that has me so concerned,'' he retorted.

She wanted to ask him what an admonition was, but she'd be damned if she'd give him the satisfaction. Besides, his sarcastic tone of voice told her everything she really needed to know about his statement.

Making a mental note to look the word up later, she told him, ''You know, if you stopped long enough to notice, you might realize that people aren't necessarily as dumb as you think they are. Just because *you* can't be bothered with simple pleasures doesn't mean simple pleasures have nothing to offer.''

He narrowed his eyes at her. "What's your point?"

She glared back at him. "Just…just…"

Just what *was* her point? she wondered. She expelled a restless puff of air that blew her bangs out of her eyes, then lifted a hand to point an accusatory finger at him. "Just that I bet *Mr.* Jamiolkowski called *Mrs.* Jamiolkowski to tell her *he'd* run into an old friend, and not to expect him for dinner."

Willis hesitated only a second before telling her, "For one thing, that segue makes no sense at all. For another thing…" He sighed heavily. "For another thing, you're not my wife, Rosemary."

She dropped her gaze back down to the floor and felt heat rush furiously into her face. She was mortified by what she'd just said, what she'd just implied, but there was no way to retract it now. So she only remained silent.

"Rosemary?"

When she glanced up, Willis was watching her with the oddest expression on his face. He looked almost as if he was…worried about her.

"What?" she asked.

"You weren't…expecting me. Were you?"

She expelled a sound that she'd intended to be dismissive, but that came out sounding distressed, instead. "Of course not."

But he looked past her, at the dishes settled in the drainer, one of which was a great, big casserole pan that a person cooking for one would never use. Rosemary deflated, and decided to just continue with the lie, however pointless.

"I wasn't expecting you," she repeated halfheartedly. "But if you're still hungry, I put the leftovers in the refrigerator."

Then, not waiting for a response, she pushed past him, wishing she could still claim at least a thread of dignity, knowing, however, that Willis Random had stripped her of that a long, long time ago.

Willis watched her go and had no idea what to say. He hadn't told Rosemary for sure that he would be joining her for dinner. Had he? He might have implied it, but surely he hadn't promised. He couldn't remember now. But doubtless she wouldn't have gone to any extra trouble for him, regardless of whether he was there or not. Would she?

He moved quickly to the refrigerator and flung open the door, to find a collection of nearly empty shelves housing the lifeblood of a single person—a half-dozen eggs, a half gallon of skim milk, a half-full jar of olives, a half of a grapefruit and half of a single-serving yogurt six-pack. And there, on the bottom shelf, a very large bowl of salad and more than enough leftover casserole to feed a good-size scientist.

"Damn," he mumbled. She *had* gone to a lot of trouble. For him. How very odd...

Thinking back, he supposed the polite thing would have been to call her and tell her for certain that he wouldn't be at the house for dinner. An appropriate time might have been, oh...right after Mr. Jamiolkowski had called Mrs. Jamiolkowski to let *her* know he wouldn't be home. But Willis honestly hadn't thought Rosemary would be expecting him. The manner in which she had extended her invitation-offer-whatever-the-hell-it-had-been for him to join her hadn't exactly commanded an RSVP. Still, he supposed it would have been a nice gesture just to let her know for sure.

But then, acting nice around Rosemary had never been first and foremost in his mind. Being constantly treated like a beetle pinned down for dissection rather did that to a person.

Of course, she hadn't necessarily been treating him like a beetle since he'd come back to Endicott, had she? Some of the looks she'd thrown his way had been almost inviting, in a strange, adolescent, just-try-and-make-me kind of way. On the other hand, she hadn't exactly been *warm* toward her. But then, neither had he toward her.

Willis uttered a restless sound and ran a big hand through his dark hair in frustration. Why did the wounds sustained as a young man run so deep? Why couldn't he just forget about the way Rosemary had treated him in high school and act like a mature adult?

He wasn't here to patch things up with her, anyway. He was here to study a comet. Period. If Rosemary still harbored any ill will toward him, that was her problem, not his. And if he still felt an occasional pang of adolescent angst or insult, then that was something he'd have to deal with himself later, when he wasn't preoccupied by the behavior of a certain comet.

So why was he so worried now about Rosemary's feelings? Hell, it wasn't as if she'd been careful not to step on his own.

A soft meow from behind him had Willis spinning around. Isosceles sat atop the refrigerator in the shape that had inspired his name, gazing at his master curiously.

"Are you still up there?" Willis asked the animal. "You're a disgrace to your gender. Get down here this instant."

The cat eyed him warily.

"Ska is outside," he said. "She was on the front porch when I came in."

That seemed to do the trick, because Isosceles crouched on the edge of the refrigerator, made a spectacular leap to the kitchen counter, then jumped down to the floor and sauntered to his master's side as if he hadn't a care in the world. Willis noted the two bowls that had rattled together upon the cat's launch, and he softened some toward Rosemary when he realized she'd taken care of his cat in his absence.

When he removed the bowls from the top of the refrigerator, he noted with some surprise that Isosceles had consumed all but a few morsels of the plebeian kibble Willis had been certain the cat would snub. Clearly, there was no accounting for taste.

"What's gotten into you?" he muttered down to the cat. "A pretty face, and you turn to mush. You're a purebred Turkish Angora, for God's sake. You're way above that common alley cat, and don't you forget it."

Isosceles blinked his clear blue eyes, but said nothing.

"And stay away from this stuff," Willis cautioned further with a nod toward the empty bowl. "It's filler. It will do absolutely nothing for you, nutritionally speaking."

Again, Isosceles kept his opinion to himself, and, tail raised high, he left his master alone in the kitchen.

And all Willis could do was thank God and all the Fates that he, at least, was a man of science.

"Maybe you should just try to be nice to him, Rosemary."

Rosemary snapped her attention up from her coffee to glare at Kirby, wondering how severe a blow to the back of the head her friend had sustained to be spouting such nonsense. Along with Angie, the three women were awaiting the arrival of their usual desserts after one of their usual lunches together, seated at their usual table, at their usual haunt, the Maple Leaf Café.

But their conversation this afternoon had been anything *but* usual. Between Angie's recounting of the breaking-and-entering act she had committed the night before—breaking into the house of a *mobster,* no less—and Kirby's assertion that she'd just been exposed to a world-renowned millionaire playboy—exposed in the most fundamental sense of the word, in that she'd been naked at the time—Rosemary was beginning to wonder just what Bob thought he was doing on this particular trip past the planet.

Clearly, the comet was messing with at least Kirby's mind, for the other woman to have made such a boneheaded suggestion as being nice to the guy who had made Rosemary's life miserable for years.

"Be nice to Willis," she elaborated, thinking she must surely have misheard Kirby the first time.

Her friend nodded, straight shafts of pale-blond hair bobbing on her shoulders when she did. "Sure, why not? You never know. Maybe he's changed. Maybe he could be a nice guy if you put forth the first effort."

Rosemary shook her head adamantly. "Trust me. Willis hasn't changed at all." Involuntarily, she recalled the way his brief shorts had hugged a truly spectacular derriere, and she felt heat seep up from her chest into her face. "At least, not inside," she amended.

"So what's he look like now?" Angie asked as she dumped five sugar packets into her coffee. She threw her head back as she looked up, her loose, dark-blond curls flying. "You never did tell us. Did he at least get his braces off?"

Rosemary tamped down a sigh of wistful longing. "He has beautiful teeth," she said, staring off into space as she recalled.

When she returned her attention to her companions, she saw Angie and Kirby eyeing her expectantly. "And?" they chorused as one.

"And he has beautiful eyes, too," she added, assuring herself she only imagined the dreamy quality her voice seemed to have adopted. "He must have gotten those lightweight lenses for his glasses, too, because it's not like staring at a big bug when you look at him head-on now."

Kirby and Angie nodded, then, as one, they arched their eyebrows in silent encouragement for more information.

Rosemary sighed again. "And his hair is a lot darker than it used to be. A very nice dark auburn that Miss Clairol would probably kill to be able to reproduce. His hair..." She surrendered to another sigh. "He has beautiful hair."

"And the pizza face?" Kirby asked.

"Gone. His skin is...beautiful. Willis looks..." Her voice trailed off again, but she rallied herself enough to add desperately, "God, he's gorgeous, you guys. He's big and brawny and...and beautiful. More beautiful than I ever imagined he would be. It's not fair that such a pizza-faced little twerp should grow up to be that smart *and* that good-looking. He should have to pay for something *some*where along the line."

Kirby shook her head slowly. "Boy, you've got it bad, Rosemary."

Rosemary eyed her friend warily, refusing to believe that Kirby was suggesting what she was suggesting. Because if she was, then it went way beyond comet-induced boneheadedness and straight into the confinement-to-a-padded-cell department.

Nevertheless, she asked her friend, "What do you mean by that?"

Kirby chuckled. "Look at you. Listen to the way you talk about Willis. You act like you're halfway gone on the guy."

Rosemary stiffened. "I am *not* gone—halfway or otherwise—on Willis Random. He's barely been in town twenty-four hours, for crying out loud.'' She nibbled her lip thoughtfully for a moment before adding, ''If anything, I might, maybe, perhaps, possibly, potentially be kind of, sort of, a little bit…'' She rushed the rest of the statement past her lips as quickly as she could. ''Under the influence of Bob.''

''What?'' Kirby asked.

''You heard me,'' Rosemary said quietly. ''If I happen to be a little, um…preoccupied now and then by thoughts of Willis, oh, say…wrapped in a towel—''

''You've been thinking about Willis Random wrapped in a towel?'' Kirby squeaked incredulously.

''Then it's only because of Bob,'' Rosemary finished, ignoring her friend's question. ''Clearly Bob has entered his sphere of influence and has started digging into his little bag of tricks, messing with the heads of the good people of Endicott, one of whom happens to be me. That's all there is to it.''

Kirby eyed her friend suspiciously. ''Do you really believe in that myth about the comet affecting people's behavior?''

''I do,'' Angie volunteered before Rosemary had a chance to answer.

''Really?'' Kirby asked.

''Well, yeah,'' Angie said, as if those who *didn't* buy into the suggestion of the comet's influence were the ones who were oddballs. ''Don't you?''

Kirby seemed to give that some thought for a minute. ''I don't know. I've never felt that weird when Bob came around.''

''Kirb,'' Angie said, ''I broke into a criminal's house last night. Rosemary here is dreaming about Willis Random in a towel. Now don't you think that kind of behavior is a mite bit weird, even for us?''

Again, Kirby pondered the question posed her. ''I still don't know if I'm convinced.''

''Well, I am,'' Angie stated flatly. She turned to her other companion. ''Rosemary, don't worry about it. Just go with the flow for now. In a couple of weeks, Bob will be on his way out, and you'll be back to hating Willis in no time."

A flicker of hope sparked in Rosemary's midsection. "You think so?"

"I guarantee it. This is just Bob playing one of his tricks. Mark my words. Two weeks," she reiterated. "Three at the outside. Then you'll be back to feeling the way you felt about him in high school."

Kirby sipped her coffee, then settled the cup back down in her saucer with a soft *clink*. "Now that you mention it, though," she said, "just what *did* you feel for Willis back in high school?"

This time Rosemary was the one to chuckle, but there wasn't an iota of good cheer in the sound. "What are you talking about?" she asked. "I loathed Willis in high school. I hated him. I despised him. I wanted his head on a spit. You know that."

"Maybe...but I think there was more to it than that," Kirby said. "Nobody could hate somebody as much as you and Willis hated each other without there being more to it than that."

"She's right," Angie concurred. "You two did always seem to go after each other with an awful lot of steam. Most people who were sworn enemies would just avoid each other. You guys were always at each other's throats."

"He was my lab partner," Rosemary reminded them. "I couldn't have avoided him if I'd tried."

"Yeah," Angie said, "but some of your more spectacular flare-ups happened in places other than chemistry class. I remember a certain homecoming dance where you and Willis went at it like baking soda and vinegar."

"Oh, wow, I forgot about that," Kirby said. "Remember, Rosemary? When Willis told you your dress looked like something out of *Night of the Living Dead?*"

"I remember," she replied tightly. How could she have forgotten that?

"And there was that one time at the pool," Kirby added, "when Willis snapped your bikini top and called you a simpleminded, slack-brained know-nothing, and you picked him up and threw him into the deep end—remember that? You wound up having to jump in after him and rescue him, because he couldn't swim.''

Rosemary did indeed remember the episode—all too well. Willis had made her pay for that one for months afterward, belittling her intelligence, her femininity, her very existence on the planet every single time she encountered him. She supposed it *had* been kind of humiliating for him to be rescued by the person he'd attacked—especially when that person was a girl, and a sworn enemy at that—but he'd started it.

Come to think of it, he'd almost always started it, she recalled now. She *had* always tried to stay out of Willis's way when she could. Hey, who went looking for someone who always ended up making her feel stupid? Willis had always been the one who seemed to scope her out and pick a fight with her.

"Yes, I remember," she told Kirby softly. "But there's no way I could pick Willis up and throw him in a pool these days. No matter how badly I might want to."

She saw her two friends exchange looks, then Kirby reiterated, "You've got it bad, all right. Bob or no Bob, something tells me part of you isn't all that upset to see Willis back in town after all these years."

Rosemary gaped at her. "You've got to be kidding. The *last* person I'd want to turn up in my life these days is Willis Random."

"I don't know," Kirby added dubiously. "I seem to remember a night fifteen years ago when you wished upon a comet that Willis Random would get what was coming to him someday."

Gee, she had sort of wished that, hadn't she? Rosemary remembered now. But she'd just been a kid when she'd sent that wish skyward. Back then, in addition to thinking Bob affected people's behavior, she'd also believed in the myth of the wishes. But now that she was a mature woman, she knew it took more than a simple wish upon a comet to make dreams come true. Now that she was a mature woman, she knew dreams *didn't* come true. Because if they did, her life would have turned out a whole lot different from what it was now.

"Yeah, that's right," Angie agreed. "Now that Kirby mentions it, it seems to me you should have been looking forward to Willis's return as much as you would Bob's, just to make sure your wish came true and that Willis *did* get what he had coming to him." She paused a telling beat, then met Rosemary's gaze levelly as she added, "Whatever that 'what' might be."

Kirby nodded. "You certainly seem to be awfully anxious about something."

"Well, of course I'm anxious," Rosemary defended herself. "How would *you* feel to be standing in your kitchen—in your underwear, no less—minding your own business, only to have some gorgeous guy show up in the doorway ogling you, a gorgeous guy who turned out to be someone who'd always hated your guts and whose guts you'd always hated in return?"

Then she remembered something her friend had mentioned earlier in their conversation that afternoon. "Then again," she began, eyeing Kirby with interest, "you said a little while ago that James Nash saw you naked, didn't you? But you never really elaborated on that."

Immediately, Kirby straightened, and the temperature at the table seemed to drop fifty degrees. Earlier that afternoon, just as Rosemary had been about to announce that she'd booked rooms in Endicott for James Nash, the internationally known and widely lusted-after playboy-millionaire-eccentric-amateur astronomer and comet watcher, Kirby had piped up that she'd already met the man, and that he'd seen her naked.

It had been a revelation of monumental proportions, not just because meeting James Nash was the equivalent of an Elvis sighting for some people, but because of the fact that no man in Endicott had ever seen Kirby naked before. Not that she hadn't tried.

"Didn't it make *you* a little anxious to be caught...off guard...so to speak?" Rosemary taunted her friend.

"That's totally different," Kirby said with an indignant sniff.

"In what way?" Rosemary challenged.

"James Nash is a complete stranger. Not to mention a promiscuous, playboy Peeping Tom. Willis is…is…"

"A pain in the butt," Rosemary finished uncharitably. "That's what he is. He always has been, and he always will be."

"I still think you should try to be nice to him," Kirby told her, clearly jumping at the chance to change the subject. "Who knows? Maybe you and Willis will wind up actually liking each other."

"I sincerely doubt that."

"Well, it's worth a shot. At least it might keep you from getting an ulcer from being around Willis while you're waiting for Bob to make his exit."

Rosemary sighed wearily. Was it really worth the effort? she wondered. She'd never tried being nice to Willis before, so she had no idea how he'd reciprocate. What if she did make a nice overture toward him, and then he threw it back up in her face? She'd just wind up feeling foolish. Then again, as long as she and Willis were adversaries, she was going to wind up feeling foolish, no matter what.

He was just way out of her league, intellectually speaking. He could rattle off a recipe for chocolate-chip cookies and make her feel that she had no idea what he was talking about. Then again, she'd never been good in the kitchen, either.

Rosemary dropped her head into her hands and wished she would wake up from what was nothing more than a bad dream. But where Willis Random was concerned, her life had always been a nightmare, so that wasn't likely to happen.

"Just give it a try, Rosemary," Kirby cajoled. "Maybe all it will take is a nice gesture on your part to mend the rift that's separated you and Willis for half your lives. At least it would make the next few weeks easier to get through."

"Yeah," Angie piped up. "What have you got to lose?"

What *did* she have to lose? Rosemary asked herself. What would it cost her to be nice to Willis for once in her life? To treat him like a human being instead of pizza-faced little twerp? To give him the benefit of the doubt? For all she knew, maybe the two of them *could* be friends, if they just gave it a try. As much as Bob was messing with her head, maybe the comet would mess with Willis's, too, and do something to improve his disposition.

"Okay," she relented. "I'll be nice to him. Once. But if he doesn't come around that one time, I'm not going to set myself up again. You ask me, once a pizza-faced little twerp, always a pizza-faced little twerp."

"People change," Angie said. "Give him a chance."

"I'll give him *one,*" Rosemary said adamantly. "But no more than that."

And even with that small concession, she felt her heart rate quicken. Willis had better be nice to her in return, she thought. Because if he wasn't, then the little skirmishes they'd fought so far were going to blow up into one full-scale war with global repercussions.

Damn the torpedoes and full speed ahead.

Four

Willis tugged the shirttail of his olive-drab T-shirt from the waistband of his khaki shorts and used it to dry the perspiration that had formed on his glasses. Then he wiped his sweaty forehead with his shoulder and sleeve and raked his fingers through his damp hair. Donning his spectacles once more, he took a few steps backward and observed his handiwork.

His telescope had arrived in Endicott that morning—almost exactly twenty-four hours after he himself had, and in roughly a million pieces. Once he'd finished unpacking his personal effects in Rosemary's spare bedroom, he had hauled the crates and cartons up to her attic, one by tedious one, and had spent the better part of his day inserting tab A into slot B. By the time she arrived home from work, the instrument was completely assembled, cleaned, positioned, plugged in and ready for action.

Now all he needed was Bobrzynyckolonycki.

The comet wouldn't be visible to the naked eye for about another week, but if his calculations were correct—and, naturally, his calculations were *always* correct—he should be able to view Bobrzynyckolonycki in the scope sometime that night or the one following. He'd already observed the comet's approach to the earth from the big telescope at MIT's Haystack Observatory in Westford, and had collected as much data as he could. Now, even though this telescope was smaller, he should be able to learn even more. It was only a matter of time before he pinned down Bobrzynyckolonycki once and for all.

He could scarcely believe it was finally happening. For fifteen years, the comet had called to him from the cosmos, and for fifteen years, Willis had been readying himself for Bobrzynyckolonycki's return. The last time he had tangled with the comet, he had only been a boy with a limited knowledge of such things. This time, however...

This time he was a man fully grown, a man well schooled in the study of celestial bodies, a man who had been around the universe a time or two, thank you very much. This time, Willis was going to take on Bobrzynyckolonycki and have his way with the comet, as he had always fantasized about doing. This time, he was going to get to the bottom of the comet's intentions. This time, he would be the one in charge of the situation, the one calling the shots, the one who wound up on top. He could feel the promise of fulfillment humming in his veins already.

Wow, was it hot up here, or what? he thought suddenly, tugging at the damp collar of his T-shirt.

Rosemary's attic was well suited to his needs for a variety of reasons. In addition to the conveniently placed windows, the flooring was solid oak capable of withstanding the weight of a large telescope. And even with the scope in place, there was plenty of room for Willis to move around. Rosemary didn't have much to store, evidently, aside from some open cardboard boxes full of notebooks, scrapbooks, yearbooks and other memorabilia, boxes he had taken it upon himself to shove to the other side of the room.

He'd set up a makeshift office in the opposite corner, near the telescope, complete with a collapsible desk and chair, and had stacked his textbooks, notebooks and celestial charts around the portable furniture. And in addition to the overhead lighting, there were enough electrical outlets for his laptop, an extra reading lamp and the telescope itself.

But the best thing about Rosemary's attic was that it put distance—physical distance, at any rate—between him and her. There was little chance she would have cause to join him up here, and with her staying out of his way, Willis would be infinitely more capable of doing his job. The last thing he needed right now was to have his hormones worked into a twist by some latent adolescent lust for a woman who understood his life's work about as well as a golden retriever would.

The rapid *thump-thump-thump* of footsteps echoed on the hardwood stairs below, alerting him to Rosemary's arrival. But he expected she would bypass the collapsible attic steps extended down into the middle of her hallway and ignore the fact that he was around. She'd barely mumbled a "Good morning" to him when he'd encountered her in the kitchen before she left for work.

Of course, he'd been so overcome by memories of her standing there in her underwear twenty-four hours earlier that she could have snapped his thigh with a wet towel and he wouldn't have noticed. This morning, she'd been dressed again in her work uniform of stark-white shirt and navy blue skirt that, for some reason, Willis found profoundly erotic. Then again, he thought, ashamed of himself, Rosemary March could be dressed in a beekeeper suit and he'd still be turned on. She'd been a sexpot at fifteen, and she was a sexpot at thirty. She would arouse any man who was at least semiconscious.

Dammit.

"Willis?" she called from the foot of the attic steps. "Are you up there?"

"Yes," he called in return, settling his glasses back in place and tamping down the errant thoughts that danced around in his head.

Within seconds, her head popped up through the square hole in the attic floor, followed quickly by her upper body. Without warning, his stomach clenched convulsively. She was so beautiful, he noted yet again. Just as she had been back in high school. A magnificent shell that, for all intents and purposes—*his* intents and purposes, at any rate—housed a mind that held absolutely no appeal. He still didn't understand how he could want Rosemary March as badly now as he had when he was a kid.

Normally, his sexual appetite paled in comparison to his hunger for learning. But with Rosemary, the quest for knowledge went right out the window, and all he wanted to explore, instead, was her. Every last inch of her. Slowly and methodically, with all the attention due an extensive study. Preferably while she was naked.

She settled her elbows on the floor and surveyed the scene, then whistled low. "Wow. You've really done a lot of work today."

He nodded, squelching his rampant fantasies as best he could. "I hope you don't mind. I rearranged things up here a bit."

"No, I don't mind at all." She glanced over at the boxes he had moved to the other side of the room. "I honestly don't even remember what's stored up here. When I moved into the house, I just took all the stuff from my hall closet in the apartment and brought it up to the attic. A lot of it is leftovers from when I was a kid, I think."

She returned her gaze to him, and her eyes widened at the contraption beside him. "So that's your big feat of engineering."

Willis couldn't help but feel proud. "This is it. The Random telescope. A telescope of revolutionary design, friend of astronomers, astrophysicists and cosmologists everywhere. Patent pending," he added with a smile.

She smiled back. "Looks pretty complicated."

"It is."

When he didn't elaborate, her smile fell some, and Willis wondered why. Rosemary wouldn't understand how the telescope worked, and really, why would she care? But when she pushed herself up through the attic door and strode toward him, she seemed a little deflated somehow. And he could see as she studied the monstrosity from a few steps away that she wanted to ask him something. But she remained silent.

"What?" he asked. "Did you want to say something?"

She shook her head. "No."

Liar, he thought. Her dark eyes were lit up like two little Christmas trees. She was *very* impressed by his big instrument, he thought. She just didn't want to let on. She was probably afraid he might think she actually wanted to learn more about it. About him. Or that she even wanted to experience his tool for herself firsthand. God forbid she should show any kind of interest in him *or* his instrument.

Or maybe she was just afraid he'd shoot down any question she might ask, with a sarcastic retort manufactured to make her feel like an idiot.

The thought materialized in his brain without warning, and Willis quickly pushed it aside. No retort from him was necessary to illustrate Rosemary March's ignorance where things scientific were concerned. She managed that all by herself. By constantly belittling his chosen field of study, she did a fine job on her own of looking the fool.

But at the moment, something about his work did fascinate her—it didn't take a rocket scientist to figure that out. She started to place a hand gingerly on the scope of the big machine, but stopped and threw a startled look at Willis first, as if asking permission.

"Go ahead," he told her, oddly thrilled that she would be so interested. "You can touch it."

She curled her fingers carefully over the cylinder, brushing them up and down the length of the long, thick shaft. Something inside Willis knotted tightly as he watched her perform the action, and he felt a part of himself rousing to life that had no business being roused.

"It's so *big*," Rosemary said softly, reverently.

"Yes," he agreed, hoping he only imagined the strangled little sound that punctuated the word. "It is."

"I can't believe it's yours," she added.

"Oh, it's mine, all right."

She covered the scope more confidently with her hand, ran

her palm slowly along the entire length of it, down to its base, then gently fingered each of the knobs she encountered there. Willis bit back a groan as he watched her, telling himself there was absolutely nothing about her actions to warrant the leap of unabashed heat that pooled in his groin at the sight.

It was just that Rosemary was such a sexy woman, he told himself. Anything she did was bound to wreak lusty havoc with his libido.

"Wow, Willis," she said softly. "This is really amazing."

"Thank you," he managed to get out. He cleared his throat awkwardly before adding, "I'm glad you like it."

"Oh, yeah. I like it a lot."

Something inside him wrung itself even more tightly, and for the life of him, he couldn't think of a single intelligent thing to say. So he just gazed at her, noted the beauty and elegance of her profile, and the way the sunlight streaming through the open window celebrated the golden highlights in her dark, riotously curly hair. The warm breeze stirred a few of those curls as he watched, then blew open the collar of her shirt. Beneath it, a breath of white lace peeked out at him from inside. Willis felt his fingers twitch involuntarily, then he forced himself to look away.

"Boy, you've really done a lot with your life since we graduated from high school, haven't you?" she asked softly.

When he glanced back at her again, she was gazing at him full on. A tentative little smile curled her full lips, and her eyes glistened with warmth.

"I suppose I've accomplished one or two things," he agreed noncommittally.

She shook her head almost imperceptibly, as if she were just now considering something she hadn't considered before. "There's nothing at all of the boy left in you anymore, is there?"

He squeezed his eyes shut tight at the question, his libido jumping to life again the moment she voiced it. No, there was nothing at all of the boy left in him, he thought. Nothing except an undying carnal longing for one Rosemary March that he would never be able to understand or pursue.

Hastily, he stripped his eyeglasses from his face, fishing in his pocket for a handkerchief. For some reason, his glasses had become all sweaty again, so he rubbed furiously at the damp lenses. Without his glasses, Rosemary was thrown into a hazy blur, and he was oddly thankful for the distortion. Surely a blur couldn't be sexy. Surely a blur couldn't unleash a storm in his libido.

Unfortunately, the memory of her touching his telescope so intimately could—and it did. And Willis was helpless to stop the groan that wound through him. Instead of replacing his glasses, he folded the earpieces down on each other and stuck them into his T-shirt pocket. Okay, so now he was blind, he thought. Hadn't he always been told as a boy that if he did *that* long enough, blindness would be the result?

He shook his head to empty it of its bizarre thoughts, then cleared his throat in an effort to steady his voice. Unfortunately, there was little he could do about other parts of his body as long as Rosemary was in the same zip code. So he gritted his teeth hard and sat down.

"Really," she told him, her voice dropping a few decibels. "I mean, maybe we got off to a rocky start yesterday, but ever since I saw you again, I've just been so impressed by the man you've become."

He eyed her hazy silhouette suspiciously, thinking maybe he should have kept his glasses on, because it was impossible to gauge the facial expression of a blur. Why was she being nice to him all of a sudden? Was she setting him up for a fall?

"What do you mean by that?" he asked her.

In spite of his nearsightedness, he could tell she dropped her gaze to the floor, as if she were ashamed about what she was going to tell him.

"Just that you grew up and did everything you said you were going to do," she murmured softly. "You've really made something of yourself. You'll be leaving your mark on history, just like you always said you would."

Still wary, he responded, "I haven't yet. I still have to come up with some explanation for why Bobrzynyckolonycki behaves the way it does."

"No, you don't."

Her assertion stumped him. "I don't?"

She looked back up at him, and he very much wished he could see her face. But to don his glasses now might make her misconstrue his actions. She might think he did it because he wanted to get a better look at her. Okay, so that wouldn't exactly be misconstruing his actions, he conceded. But he didn't want her to think he actually placed any kind of importance on what she was saying. Even if he did.

"No, you don't," she assured him. "You've designed this telescope. It's awesome, Willis. Whether you figure out Bob or not, you've done something that's going to make a lot of people remember you."

"Only a lot of other astronomers, astrophysicists and cosmologists," he noted. "The general public won't know me from Adam."

"Yeah, but what do you care? You don't like the general public anyway."

What she said was true, of course, Willis told himself. So why did it bother him to hear her say it? He *had* reserved himself a place in history—scientific history, at any rate—by designing his telescope. But for some reason, that wasn't enough. He wanted everyone to know his name. Not just other scientists—*everyone*. But then, why would that be the case, if he had no use for people other than scientists?

Suddenly feeling puzzled and angry for some reason, Willis bit out, "Just forget it. You wouldn't understand, Rosemary."

She dropped her gaze down to the floor again. "No, I guess I wouldn't, would I?" she said sadly. "Hey, I'm just a simpleminded, slack-brained know-nothing, after all, aren't I?"

The words hit Willis like a prizefighter's fist to his belly. Simpleminded. Slack-brained. Know-nothing. That was what he had always called her back in high school. He'd forgotten all about that until she brought it up again. But obviously, Rosemary hadn't forgotten about it at all. And again, he wished he could see her face.

But by the time he had his glasses back in place, she had

spun around and was striding quickly toward the attic stairs. "Rosemary," he called out after her.

She hesitated just before stepping down, and cast a cautious look over her shoulder. "What?"

"I..." He what? he wondered. How did a grown man apologize for being a stupid kid more than a decade after the fact? He sighed heavily. "Never mind."

She turned around again, but her voice carried back to him one more time. "Will you be here for dinner tonight?"

He could be, he knew. He hadn't made any plans at all. But he told her, "No, I'll be out. I have to go into town for a few things, and I thought I'd just grab a bite while I'm there."

She nodded. "Okay." And then she disappeared down through the attic door.

And all Willis could do was look at the empty hole in the floor and wonder why it reminded him so much of what he was feeling inside.

Hours later, he was gazing at that hole again as if mesmerized by it. He had moved to sit on the attic floor opposite his telescope, beside the window that wasn't blocking what little evening breeze was available. The cavernous room was hot, though not unbearably so, and he turned his face away from the attic door to enjoy what little air stirred into the big room from outside.

Beyond the gaping window, now free of its slats, the thin slice of a waning moon hung high amid what looked to be billions of stars. Crickets and katydids chorused loudly, almost drowning out the strains of Mussorgsky rattling the speakers of his portable stereo. Yet he could still detect the whisper of the wind as it whiffled through the black treetops right at his eye level.

Nighttime in Endicott was every bit as peaceful and soothing as he remembered. He glanced down at his watch to find that it was nearly 3 a.m. He still couldn't quite make out Bobrzynyckolonycki through the lens of his telescope as well as he needed to in order to start gathering data, so he'd been spending his time gazing upon other galactic sights that caught his fancy, instead. But now even that pastime had grown tiresome, so he was taking a little break.

As he lowered his hand back down to the floor, his gaze lit on the stacks of boxes he had placed there the day before. On top of one was an old scrapbook with a picture of a big-eyed kitten holding a flower in its mouth, gaggingly sweet-looking in its portrayal. Idly, Willis lifted the scrapbook and began to flip through the pages, shaking his head and smiling at the collection of childhood innocence it contained. Photographs of little girls giggling at birthday parties, of camp-outs with the Girl Scouts, of melting ice cream on sunny summer days. Rosemary and her friends Angie and Kirby—whom Willis remembered well from school—grinned at him from each and every picture.

He closed and replaced the scrapbook, then glanced at the contents of the box sitting beside it, and found the 1985 edition of the Endicott Central *Beehive* stacked right on top. Good God—the yearbook from his senior year of high school. He hadn't even ordered one for himself, simply because he hadn't wanted any record of that period of his life to remind him of how unhappy he had been. But he couldn't resist a peek into the past now, and before he even realized he was doing it, he cracked open the faded gold, leather-bound annual with the fighting yellowjacket on its front.

Color photos of the senior play assaulted him, carrying him backward in time thirteen years at warp speed. *South Pacific*. Rosemary had played Bloody Mary's daughter, and had spent the entirety of the play dressed in a skimpy little island girl costume that had driven him half-mad. Willis had been part of the technical crew, and had spent the entirety of the play standing behind a spotlight way up high in the bleachers of the gym.

Everyone at Central had wondered that year why Rosemary had always seemed to glow amid a pool of soft light, no matter where she was onstage. Everyone, of course, except Willis.

He smiled at the memory and flipped through a few more pages, stopping when he reached the color gallery of the members of the senior class. He located his own image first, and shook his head in wonder at the boy he had been. Even to his own eyes, the picture of a fifteen-year-old Willis was homely and ungainly. Truly a face only a mother could love.

Beneath his name, his list of credits was long and impressive—at least it had been to the admissions board of MIT. The student body of Endicott Central, however, had considered things like Chemistry Club, Physics Club, Chess Club, Latin Club, Beta Club, National Honor Society, National Merit Scholar, and on and on and on, unworthy of social recommendation.

Thumbing back two pages, he found Rosemary's likeness, then caught his breath at the image gazing back at him from the photograph. Her hair had been much longer then, her dark curls spilling down around the bare shoulders revealed by the thin straps of her sundress. Her dark eyes fairly sparkled, and her lips were parted in a smile redolent of confidence and happiness. Her complexion, he noted, was flawless.

The credits beneath her name went on endlessly, too, and were the kind that guaranteed cachet into high school popularity—cheerleader, senior class secretary, senior chorus, Spanish Club, Drama Club, and all the other chic adolescent societies.

Willis shook his head in wonder that he and Rosemary hadn't spontaneously combusted like matter and antimatter upon their first meeting.

As he fanned quickly through a few more pages, he noted the assortment of signatures that Rosemary had collected in the yearbook. It appeared that she had asked everyone in the senior class to sign her annual. Everyone except Willis, of course. And all of her friends had penned good wishes and recalled fond memories, and had written down things like "I'll always remember your smile" and "Stay as sweet as you are" and "Did we have fun, or what?" and "2Good+2Be=4Gotten."

Willis fumbled for the pocket of his T-shirt and withdrew the black felt-tip pen that habitually resided there. Gripping the cap in his teeth, he tugged it off, then turned to the very back of the yearbook and found a tiny, tiny place without a signature. And before he could succumb to second thoughts, he scribbled in small letters "To Rosemary, whose beauty warms a winter day, whose smile illuminates the darkness and whose brain will always remain both a mystery and a marvel to me. Willis Random."

Then he capped the pen again, snapped the yearbook shut and tossed it back into the box. Only then did he realize how rapidly his heart was pounding, and how much warmer the attic seemed to have grown in a matter of minutes. He glanced back down at the yearbook again and wondered what had come over him to make him pen such a sentiment inside it.

Maybe he just wanted to make sure Rosemary remembered him, he thought. Someday, years from now, maybe she'd come up to the attic and begin to dig through her old things, and she'd pick up her senior yearbook and wander through it much as he just had. And maybe she'd see the entry from Willis Random, and wonder how he'd snatched her annual while she wasn't looking, to scrawl a sentiment inside it.

And maybe, just maybe, he thought further, when that day came, she'd read the entry he had inscribed. And when she did, maybe she would discover that her feelings for Willis were every bit as muddled and confusing as his for her had always been.

And maybe, just maybe, she would understand why he had said and done the things he had all those years ago.

Okay, Rosemary had done as her friends had asked her to do—she had tried to be nice to Willis. Thanks to whatever temporary insanity had made her agree to it—doubtless, that, too, was due to Bob's interference—she had put forth a genuine effort to behave politely toward him. She had tried to say some nice things now to make up for all the mean things she had said to him when they were teenagers. She had thrown down a white flag to see if he would pick it up. And instead, he had ground it into the dust with the toe of his big, fat hiking boot.

Fine.

She plopped down onto her sofa with a pint of chocolate-peanut butter ice cream and fumbled around under the throw pillows for the remote control. Four days had passed since she'd made her overture toward Willis, and she was still smarting from his blatant dismissal of both her and her attempt to reach out to him.

Of course, there had been his blatant dismissal of her intelligence, too, she recalled indignantly, but then, that hadn't really come as a surprise, had it? Even if by some wild miracle the two of them did manage to make up and play nicely together, Willis would always think she was stupid.

You wouldn't understand, Rosemary.

The words echoed in her head relentlessly, and she wondered why they hurt so much. No, she probably wouldn't understand how Willis's big brain worked. She would never be able to fathom all the scientific mumbo jumbo that he absorbed so effortlessly. And, truth be told, she really didn't have any desire to learn. She simply didn't have much interest in science—so sue her. But that didn't mean she had nothing to offer anyone. She just didn't have anything to offer Willis. Still, it would have been nice if he had at least appreciated her attempt to reach out to him.

It would have been nice if he'd tried being nice to her in return.

She hadn't bothered to make another foray up to her attic since then, and he hadn't bothered to join her for dinner. Nor had either of them made an effort to be civil to each other on those very few occasions when they did meet up in the house.

Hey, Willis had had his chance, she decided, and he'd blown it. As far as Rosemary was concerned, the war waged on. They hadn't liked each other in high school, and they didn't like each other now. What was the point in denying it, just because they had allegedly matured? Big sexy chest and blue eyes aside, he just wasn't a man to care deeply about. Lust after, sure. Care about? No way. Even a galactic interference wouldn't make her do something that stupid. Rosemary might be a lot of things, but a hypocrite wasn't one of them.

For the rest of his stay in her home, she intended to simply avoid Willis as best she could. So far, that hadn't posed much of a problem, because he'd been working for most of the night and sleeping during most of the day. By the time she rose for work in the morning, he had gone to bed, and when she came home in the evening, he was hard at work up in the attic. Oh, he came down once or twice a night to raid the kitchen or make phone calls, but all in all, the two of them led blissfully separate lives.

When Ska leaped up to join her on the couch, Rosemary eyed the cat suspiciously. "You've been scarce lately," she said pointedly. "Care to enlighten me as to where you've been spending your time the past couple nights? You certainly haven't been sleeping in *my* bed."

Ska stretched easily and fell back onto her haunches, then tossed her mistress one of those that's-for-me-to-know-and-you-to-find-out cat expressions with which feline lovers everywhere are so familiar.

"Hmpf," Rosemary grumbled. "You just better not be making time with Isosceles," she warned the cat. "That guy's no good for you. You deserve much better than that big know-it-all, Science Diet-scarfing geek of a feline. He'll only break your heart."

Lifting her right paw to give it an idle wash, Ska seemed unconcerned.

Rosemary mumbled another warning to Ska about the dangers of succumbing to the tomcat's blue eyes, then snatched up the *TV Guide* and scanned the late-night entries. Then she tossed it aside again and channel-surfed until she hit upon the opening credits for *The Tomb of Ligeia*. Oh, boy. Roger Corman. This ought to be good. And she should know—she'd seen the movie at least a half-dozen times already. She turned off the lamp beside her, throwing the living room into total darkness outside the flickering bluish glow of the TV, and then snuggled deeper into the overstuffed sofa, hugging her ice cream to her chest.

Halfway through the film, sometime around 1 a.m., just when Vincent Price was achieving the ultimate of spooky weirdness, Willis came into the living room without a sound, leaned over the back of the sofa, uttered Rosemary's name softly...

And scared the bejabbers out of her.

As she leaped up from the couch with a shriek that could wake the dead, Ska hurtled herself to the floor and fled, and Willis stumbled backward, eyes wide, as if he were being pursued by banshees.

"What?" he barked. "What the hell is the matter?"

She clutched at her heart and gasped for breath, closing her eyes in an effort to steady her pulse rate. Beneath the fabric of her yellow, knee-length nightshirt, the one emblazoned with the words *Travel agents do it around the world,* her heart pummeled her breast bone so hard she feared it would burst from her chest.

"Jeez," she gasped. "What on earth were you trying to do? Give me a heart attack?"

Willis, too, seemed to be trying hard to calm himself down, because his own chest rose and fell with rapid respiration. "No," he muttered. "I was just wondering if you had any spare batteries."

"B-b-b-batteries?" she repeated, still shaking.

He nodded. "I need them for my calculator. I seem to have neglected to pack any extras."

She inhaled another deep breath and pointed toward the kitchen. "If I do have any—and that's a big *if*—then they'll be in the drawer by the refrigerator."

"Which one?" he asked. "Upper or lower?"

She tried to remember and realized she wasn't sure. One was the junk drawer—the one that housed things she was pretty sure were absolutely inessential, but that looked as if they just might have some purpose in life at some point, so she couldn't quite bring herself to throw them out—and the other was the *faux*-junk drawer—the one where she put things she was quite certain had some use, but that she couldn't honestly ever see herself needing very often. Like batteries. However, it wasn't uncommon for things to get switched from one drawer to the other, so any potential batteries could really be in either place.

Trying to explain all that to Willis, however, would doubtless take longer than actually mounting the search herself, so she told him, "I'll look."

She padded barefoot through the dining room and toward the kitchen, where a single fluorescent bulb above the kitchen sink, sputtering spasmodically, afforded the only light. That particular sight coming right on the heels of a film about the undead made her feel more than a little trepidation about entering the grotesquely lit room, and she hesitated at the door. Whereupon Willis, evidently following her more closely than she realized, bumped right into her, and she went sailing forward.

Until he reached out and caught her wrist in his hand.

Then Rosemary felt herself being pulled backward and reeled into a massive chest. Instinctively, she lifted her hands to buffer the impact, and found herself with her fingers splayed open over that magnificent collection of muscles. Beneath the soft fabric of his white T-shirt, bumps and ridges of sinew and warm flesh greeted her fingertips, and for one wild moment, all she could do was stand there and enjoy herself.

Willis had definitely been taking good care of himself since he'd left Endicott, she marveled. Never in her life had she encountered a more perfectly formed man.

Not that she'd been this close to that many men. Not as an adult woman, anyway. Oh, sure, she'd had her fair share of boyfriends in high school, some with very nice physiques. But what good was a great male physique when you were a teenager, uncertain exactly what to do with it? Rosemary may not have been the brightest girl in her class, but she'd been smart enough to stay away from intimacy she'd been too young to handle back then.

And as a grown woman who did have some working knowledge of intimacy, there hadn't been many available men out there for her to study. Okay, she'd seen a couple of pretty decent chests in her time as a grown woman. But not like this one. Never like this one.

The collar of Willis's T-shirt was stretched out at the neck, offering her a peek of dark, coiling hair at the base of his throat. She skimmed her gaze upward, along the strong column of his neck, the line of his rough jaw and his exquisitely formed chin, lingering at the full curve of his lower lip. Wow. Willis sure did have some mouth on him, she thought. And it was so close to hers right now. *So* close. So close she could—

"Rosemary?"

Her fantasy fizzled before it picked up steam, but she still marveled at the smooth motion of his mouth when it formed her name. She swallowed against the lump that knotted her throat and asked absently, "Hmm?"

"Are you all right?"

She nodded slowly, her gaze still fixed on his mouth, a warm ripple of delight echoing through her at the deep, mellow timbre of his voice. And all she was able to offer in reply was "Mmm-hmm."

"Then I think you can let go of me now."

Gradually, his statement tugged at her attention. She directed her gaze back down to his chest, where she found her own traitorous hand bunching a fistful of his shirt with *much* affection. Immediately, she forced herself to release the soft fabric, then made the mistake of smoothing out the wrinkles left behind. Beneath her fingertips, his heart rate quickened, and she felt her own leap in response. But before she could ponder the strangeness of Willis's rapid pulse, he circled her wrist with sure fingers and snatched her hand away from his chest.

"The batteries?" he asked again through gritted teeth.

She felt herself blushing furiously and spun away from him as hastily as she could. *Not that, please,* she thought. *Anything but that.* Whatever else happened, she did *not* want Willis suspecting that she was developing a crush on him. Him walking around with knowledge like that in his head was the last thing she needed.

I am not developing a crush on Willis, she then assured herself yet again. *It's nothing more than a mild case of lust. That's all it is. Lust.*

And who wouldn't feel lust for such a man? she reasoned further. A man who looked like Willis simply commanded lusty thoughts. Who cared if his personality was abrasive, condescending and annoying? Lusting after someone was totally irrational, totally physical and in no way indicative of a person's intelligence. It would be stupid to fall prey to a crush on Willis. But it was perfectly normal to lust after him.

Still, she didn't want him thinking she was lusting after him, either. No sense making things more uncomfortable than they were already.

Besides, there was a very good chance that the only reason she was lusting after Willis—or developing a crush on him, for that matter—was that a blazing ball of ice and gas hurtling through the universe was wreaking havoc with the atmosphere above Endicott, Indiana. Bob was fast approaching the planet, and in a matter of days would be making his closest pass to the earth right above the spot where she was standing.

And even though she wasn't quite certain she believed all the myth that had risen up over the years about Bob, Rosemary was still open-minded enough to consider Angie's suggestion that maybe it was the comet wreaking havoc with her emotions, and not Willis.

And *that* thought, if no others parading through her brain lately, at least brought her some comfort. Just blame it on Bob, she told herself. That damned comet always had caused trouble whenever it came around.

She wrestled with the top drawer until she had it open, then shook her head in amazement at the collection of odds and ends she found inside. As she sorted through them, she felt Willis behind her, shifting restlessly, saying nothing.

"What?" she asked without turning around.

He hesitated briefly, then muttered, "I didn't say anything."

"No, but you're thinking something," she told him as she idly picked through the junk in the drawer.

Another hesitation, then, "Of course I'm thinking something. I'm always thinking something. My mind never shuts down for a minute."

"Maybe that's your problem," she said softly.

"What?"

Realizing there were no batteries in the top drawer, she

wrestled it shut again, then fought to open the bottom one, instead. But still she kept her back turned to Willis. "I said, 'Maybe that's your problem,'" she repeated.

"What's my problem?"

She sorted through the bits and pieces in the other drawer, but her attention was still focused soundly on the man standing behind her. "You need to give it a rest sometimes, Willis. Your brain, I mean. It's not good to be thinking all the time."

"I guess you'd know."

Okay, that did it. Rosemary slammed the drawer shut with all her might, then spun around and jabbed her index finger against his breastbone. Hard.

"Okay, that does it," she repeated aloud, surprising herself with the calmness of her voice when calm was the last thing she felt. She stabbed her finger against his chest a few more times to punctuate her intentions. "I have had it with you constantly belittling my intelligence. I'm not stupid, Willis. I'm not. Now knock it off or I'll...I'll..."

He smirked at her. Actually smirked. The creep.

"You'll what?" he asked.

She deflated then, not sure what she *could* do. She couldn't throw him out of her house, and she couldn't very well hole up somewhere else herself. She wasn't likely to grow a big brain like his overnight, and she'd never be able to convince him that even though she wasn't as smart as he was, she certainly wasn't ready to go back and start first grade all over again.

Nor was he likely to ever forgive her for the way she had treated him in high school. And that more than anything else, she supposed, was what really lay at the crux of Willis's contempt for her.

She dropped her hand to her side and slumped forward, feeling more tired than she ever had in her life. "Why don't you let up?" she asked him. "Why do you keep after me this way?"

A shutter dropped over his eyes, and she couldn't for the life of her tell what he was thinking. "I don't know what you're talking about."

"Oh, come on, Willis," she cajoled him. "You're a smart guy. You know exactly what I'm taking about."

He inhaled deeply, an action that seemed to make him even taller for some reason. "No, I don't."

She met his gaze levelly for a long time, refusing to back down. They eyed each other silently for several moments, until Willis finally looked away. And that's when she knew. That's when she understood that he was deliberately baiting her, deliberately keeping their animosity alive. Why, she couldn't imagine. But he was definitely going out of his way to rekindle the fire of enmity that had burned so brightly between them when they were kids. And he wanted to keep it going forever.

Suddenly feeling defenseless, she leaned back against the kitchen counter, crossed her arms over her chest and dropped her gaze to the floor. "Boy, you really do hate me, don't you?" she asked quietly.

She felt more than saw him stiffen, but he said nothing in response to her charge.

She nodded slowly, but still couldn't bring herself to glance up at him. "Look, I'm sorry for all the things I said to you in high school, all right? I was a thoughtless kid back then, and I didn't understand how much I hurt you, saying the things I did."

Well, that wasn't completely true, she thought. She knew exactly how deeply hastily thrown words could wound a person. Some of the remarks Willis had tossed her way had cut her to the core. Finally, she found the nerve to look up at him again, and when she did, she saw that he was staring not at her, but at something behind her—evidently the kitchen cupboards held infinitely more interest than she did.

"But you know, Willis," she continued, her voice dropping to an even softer tone, "I wasn't the only one who said some mean things back then. You were pretty good at hurling a few darts of your own."

Still he said nothing, only continued to gaze past her as if she wasn't even there. She shook her head slowly and sighed. What was the point? she wondered. The thing about guys like Willis—guys who had a bigger brain than they knew what to do with—once they made up their minds about something, it was next to impossible to change them. He was convinced that whatever had passed between them in high school—and whatever was going on with them now—he was the one in the right. He would never admit that he'd done anything wrong, so what was the point of expecting him to?

Rosemary sighed again, a hopeless sound. "I don't know what I could do to make it up to you," she told him quietly. "But I apologize for treating you the way I did when we were in high school."

She waited halfheartedly to see if he would apologize, too, but she wasn't surprised when he said nothing in response. So, feeling pretty much humiliated, and unable to tolerate his cold, distant silence, she mumbled another apology and pushed past him. She didn't stop running until she was upstairs in her bedroom with the door closed and locked behind her. Then she threw herself down on the bed, stared up into the darkness overhead and squeezed her eyes shut to keep the tears from falling.

Let Willis hunt for his own damned batteries, she thought. And maybe while he was looking, he might find his heart.

Five

He was such a bastard.

Willis shoved his glasses to the top of his head and rubbed his eyes fiercely. The telescope before him was exceeding his wildest expectations in the performance department; Bobrzynyckolonycki was right on track, headed straight for Endicott; the comet was coming in clearly and behaving exactly as he'd predicted it would, giving him ample opportunity to make the calculations necessary to figure the big gas ball out. And...

And he couldn't have cared less about any of those developments. Because all he saw when he stared out into the universe was the look on Rosemary March's face the night before when she'd accused him of hating her.

Boy, you really do hate me, don't you?

The quietly uttered question resounded in his brain like the crack of thunder from a violent storm. Instead of the powerful strains of Mussorgsky erupting from the portable stereo system nearby—music that always inspired him while he was studying the cosmos through the lens of a telescope—all Willis could hear was Rosemary's question rolling in his ears, over and over again.

Boy, you really do hate me, don't you?

If only he could, he thought morosely. If he could honestly hate her, it would make things so much easier for him now. But nothing could be further from the truth. If anything, he was overcome by an attraction to Rosemary March that he could neither understand nor tolerate. And to succumb to such feelings would mean opening himself up to ridicule and rejection all over again. So in self-defense, he lashed out at her. Because he simply didn't know how to deal with his feelings himself.

God, it was just like high school all over again.

Strangely, a part of him tried desperately to blame Bobrzynyckolonycki for the strange stirrings of desire that plagued him whenever Rosemary was within grabbing distance. Although he'd never bought into all the mythology that had surrounded the comet for centuries, he was worried enough now to wonder if perhaps such folklore provided the explanation he needed to understand his feelings. Bobrzynyckolonycki's last appearance over Endicott had coincided with the beginning of tenth grade, when Willis was first partnered with Rosemary, and when he'd first started to fall for her.

Hey, it could happen.

Then he reminded himself that his feelings for Rosemary had far outlasted the appearance of Bobrzynyckolonycki. Long after the comet had disappeared, Willis had continued to be turned inside out by his feelings for his lab partner. For fifteen years, to be precise, he recalled. Because once he'd been lured into Rosemary's orbit, he'd never quite managed to find his way out again. Like a satellite, his thoughts had rotated around her for a decade and a half. And Bobrzynyckolonycki or no Bobrzynyckolonycki, he was certain he'd always be attracted to her.

In spite of her own apology, he sincerely doubted Rosemary would ever forgive him for the things he'd said and done to her back then, even if he did put forth the effort to tell her he was sorry. He'd been a hurt kid in high school, and he'd thoughtlessly struck out in anger and resentment at the things he didn't understand—like his feelings for Rosemary. It had been more than a little difficult to have a major thing for someone who considered him to be, well, a pizza-faced little twerp.

Certainly, he was none of those things anymore. But for a long, long time, such had been his lot in life. As much as he wished he could, Willis simply could not forget about all the pain and confusion that had dogged his adolescent years. And Rosemary had played a substantial role in all that pain and confusion.

Still, that didn't give him license to attack her whenever he felt the sting of memories assaulting him. That didn't mean he could strike out at *her* whenever *he* started to feel the heat of that old attraction firing up again. But when she'd stumbled into the kitchen last night, and he'd reached out to right her, only to have her come reeling back into his arms... When he'd looked down to see her bunching the fabric of his T-shirt so possessively in her hand... When he'd seen her eyeing his mouth as if she were going to kiss him—something he'd surely mistaken...

Willis sighed and ran a big hand restlessly through his hair. When all those things had happened, he'd become completely and irrevocably aroused, and he'd realized that all he wanted to do was make thorough, uninhibited love to Rosemary March, right there on the kitchen floor. And because he was quite certain such a development would only lead to devastating disappointment, he'd struck out at her instead of reining himself in. Because, quite frankly, he was in no way certain that he *could* rein himself in.

He knew he owed Rosemary an apology for his behavior of the night before. Hell, he owed her an apology for a lot more than that. But there was no reason to dredge up more of the past than they already had. Maybe, if she could forgive him this one episode, they could at least go back to the tentative truce that had kept them at a tolerable arm's length since his return to Endicott.

He lowered his glasses back down over his eyes, then glanced at the enormous white cat that had made himself at home on top of one of the cartons that belonged to Rosemary. "Have you been hiding out, you big sissy?" he asked Isosceles. "I certainly haven't seen much of you the past few days."

The big cat blinked his eyes and rumbled a soft purr, then extended one paw outward, obviously unconcerned about his master's opinion.

"Looks to me like you're hiding out," Willis accused further. "Hiding out from a slip of a tabby you could take any day of the week."

Isosceles closed his eyes and said nothing.

Willis nodded. "Yeah, I guess you're right. Like master, like feline. Maybe it's time I took a little break."

He made one final inspection of the comet's approach through the telescope, jotted down a few more notations and calculations and rose from his stool. Glancing at his watch as he launched himself into a full-body stretch, he was surprised to discover that it was past midnight.

He wondered if Rosemary would be downstairs watching television, as she always seemed to be late at night. And he wondered, too, how she managed to rouse herself for work in the morning. She must be one of those people who could function on only a few hours' sleep per night.

No wonder she didn't expend much brain power.

Stop it, he told himself, frowning. Why did he continue to belittle her intelligence, even when she wasn't around, when there would be no point? Why was his brain always at the ready with some mean-spirited quip designed to make her feel small?

He sighed heavily. Probably because he was constantly trying to remind himself that falling in love with Rosemary March would be detrimental to his intellectual health. Probably because as long as he reminded himself that she had a very good reason to hate his guts, there was no danger that he would fall in love with her.

Falling in love, he repeated to himself miserably. Was he doomed to re-create in adulthood the adolescent feelings he'd embraced for her as a teenager? Surely not. At thirteen years old, boys fell in and out of love on an almost hourly basis. Grown men were above that, weren't they? They must be. Their hormonal reactions, although certainly still strong, had matured to a level where they were manageable. Hadn't they?

He couldn't possibly be falling in love with Rosemary. Love was something that happened when two people shared similar emotions, similar experiences, similar needs, similar desires. Love was the result of two souls colliding and joining and becoming one. Scientifically speaking, such a thing could only occur when those two souls shared common properties. And simply put, he and Rosemary had nothing at all in common.

Therefore, whatever remnants of emotion were left lingering inside him where she was concerned, they simply and absolutely could not be the result of love. Lust? Doubtless. Desire? Surely. Need? Hey, why not? But love? Never.

Unless...

Unless there was, perhaps, potentially, something to that old folk tale about Bobrzynyckolonycki's romantic interference with people who would normally never be attracted to each other. After all, he reminded himself again, his youthful crush on Rosemary March had coincided directly with Bobrzynyckolonycki's last pass by the planet. The comet's appearance then might explain why an otherwise brilliant thirteen-year-old had been overcome with the hots for a brainless beauty.

Then again, he thought further, there was that small matter of completely uncontrollable adolescent hormones that might have played a tiny role in that.

Nevertheless, Willis couldn't quite ignore the fact that Bobrzynyckolonycki had been a factor in the origin of his feelings for Rosemary fifteen years ago, and the comet was a factor now. Maybe, just maybe, there was some grain of legitimate truth in the myth about Bobrzynyckolonycki's romantic interference with the good townsfolk of Endicott.

Nah, he immediately countered himself. It couldn't be that. Willis was, after all, a scientist, and there was absolutely no scientific foundation for the suggestion that a comet—or any other celestial object, for that matter—influenced human behavior. No, he couldn't blame this one on Bobrzynyckkolo-nycki. As much as he might want to.

After one final arch of his back, Willis wiped his sweaty forehead with the sleeve of the navy blue T-shirt that hung unfettered over his ubiquitous khaki shorts. His hiking boots scuffed along the collapsible attic stairs as he made his way down, a sound punctuated by the distant droning of a television in the otherwise silent house. Rosemary's bedroom door was open, so he knew she wasn't sleeping. Not in there, at any rate. Quietly, he made his way downstairs to the first floor, coming to a halt at the foot of the steps.

The television was tuned to yet another low-budget horror movie, and Rosemary was sound asleep on the sofa. Her dark-green Winnie-the-Pooh-and-Tigger-too nightshirt was bunched up around her thighs, and her red socks were scrunched down around her ankles. Her espresso-colored, unruly curls fell down over her forehead, nearly into her eyes, and her lips were slightly parted as she breathed deeply in and out. An empty ice cream carton sat on the floor beside the couch, its lid appearing to have been licked clean by at least one feline tongue.

Willis approached her slowly, silently, and wondered why she seemed to spend every evening in front of the TV this way, instead of out painting the town with some tediously good-looking guy. In high school, she'd had a new boyfriend every time he'd turned around. She'd dated football players, basketball players, baseball players, track stars, the class president…just about every guy at Endicott Central had had a thing for Rosemary March. So why had she been sitting home alone every single night since Willis had come back to town?

He took a few steps closer, trying not to notice the soft curve of her calves and the creamy thighs that extended from the soft, dark-green fabric of her nightshirt. Trying and failing miserably. God, even her knees were sexy, he thought help-lessly. She didn't move at all as he approached her, even when he stood right beside the couch and hunkered down until his face was only a few inches in front of her own. Her breathing was deep and even, and she was clearly sacked out for the night.

Before he even realized he was doing it, Willis lifted a hand and brushed a few errant curls back from her forehead. She stirred some at the soft touch, but didn't wake up. One hand lay open on the cushion beside her face, and something inside him tightened, commanded him to twine her fingers with his, then pull her up from the couch and into his arms. Naturally, he didn't act on the impulse. But he couldn't quite keep himself from lightly tracing the two faint lines that bisected her palm.

Heart line and head line, he thought. At least, he was pretty sure that was what they were. His other girlfriend—the one who hadn't been an accounting major—had been interested in such things, in spite of the fact that she had been smart enough to know better. Willis looked at the two lines on Rosemary's hand again. One curved upward from the left, and the other curved downward from the right. Heart and head—and never the twain should meet, he ruminated further. Funny, that. Or maybe not so funny after all.

The heart and the head might be two organs that were vitally connected where the sustaining of life was concerned, he mused, but when emotions came into play, they separated like angry cats. Neither seemed much tuned to the other, and both acted far too independently. It was something he supposed even the most brilliant mind would never be able to explain.

All Willis really did know for certain at that moment was that Rosemary's hand was soft and warm, and he wondered if she was like that all over. More than likely, he decided at once. She'd always given him the impression of softness and warmth, despite the brittleness of her put-downs, despite the sharpness of her anger. So often when he'd been a teenager, he'd wanted nothing more than to lean into Rosemary's soft sweaters, her soft skin, her soft breasts, and separate himself completely from the dry, rigid world of scientific equation.

Such had been her effect on him back then. Somehow, the thought of sinking into the softness of Rosemary March—a girl who'd held no more allure for him beyond her obvious physical charms—had completely superseded his quest for knowledge. When he should have been contemplating logarithms and proofs, when he should have been considering the properties of quantum physics, he'd been daydreaming instead, about how her mouth would feel on his if he kissed her, and whether or not his braces would hurt her.

He heard a soft sound then, and brought his gaze up to her face. Her eyes fluttered open, vague, dreamy, warm, and her fingers curled reflexively over his. For one brief, delirious moment, Rosemary gazed at him the way he imagined she would gaze at a man who had just made slow, sweet, sensational love to her. Then her eyes focused and narrowed, her fingers released his and clenched into fists and she bolted upright on the couch.

"What do you want?" she asked, her voice rough, a subtle pink settling into her cheeks.

It took Willis a moment to find his own voice, because he was still so wrapped up in the lascivious ideas he'd been contemplating. Finally, he cleared his throat and stood. "I, uh…" he began.

Inevitably, his gaze wandered to her thighs, still nicely exposed thanks to the way her nightshirt had crept up even more when she'd pushed herself into a sitting position. As he studied her legs, she must have realized he was staring, because she suddenly shoved the fabric back down to her knees.

"Willis?" she asked again. "What are you doing down here? What do you want?"

He inhaled deeply and forced his gaze back up to her face. She was blushing even more fiercely than before, and for the life of him, he couldn't remember what he was doing standing there in her living room, watching her sleep.

"I, uh…" he began again. He met her gaze levelly, and the thought that leaped to the forefront of his brain jumped out of his mouth before he could stop it. "Why do you sit at home alone watching TV every night?"

Her dark eyes widened in surprise at the question, then her cheeks colored even more. "Well, gee whiz, Willis, I guess I just have a hard time understanding those…what do you call them…books. TV is a lot less taxing on this teensy-weensy brain of mine."

This time Willis was the one to color. Both in anger and embarrassment. "That's not what I meant."

"Oh, wasn't it."

He noted that she formed her remark as a statement, not a question. Then he pushed the thought away. "All I meant was…how come you don't…don't…"

"Don't what?" she demanded.

He'd come this far, he reminded himself. It was too late now to be worrying about how she might construe his interest, so he pushed the question out of his mouth. "How come you never have any dates?"

She reached behind herself for an oversize throw pillow and crushed it to her chest as if she needed it for a shield. "What do you care?" she asked.

"Forget it," he bit out, spinning around. "Just forget I asked."

"I think I will," she called out after him.

He didn't stop walking until he reached the foot of the stairs, where he forced his feet to halt. Dammit, he'd come down here to apologize to her, he reminded himself. And instead, he'd just hurt her feelings all over again. He pivoted back around and retraced his steps until he was standing in front of the sofa again.

"I came downstairs to apologize to you," he said softly, not quite able to meet her gaze. "I'm sorry about the way I behaved last night. I had no right to talk to you the way I did."

For a minute, she said nothing, and when he looked up at her again, she was studying him with an expression that indicated she didn't quite trust him. "You're sorry about last night?" she repeated.

He nodded mutely.

"Just last night?" she asked further. "Nothing else?"

Here was his chance, he thought. She'd just given him the opportunity to apologize for a host of other things he needed to apologize for. All he had to do was say he was sorry for being such a jerk kid back in high school. That was all he had to do. A dozen words and he'd be home free. *I'm sorry I was such a jerk kid back in high school.* Somehow he knew that if he offered Rosemary such a concession, then a big wide world of wonder would open up for both of them to explore. They could investigate as adults the heat that had burned between them when they were kids. And maybe, just maybe, they'd start to understand it.

But instead of offering those dozen words of apology, Willis only gazed at her in silence. He just wasn't sure he wanted to investigate—let alone understand—whatever it was that had always lurked between him and Rosemary. Because whatever he felt for her, he was fairly certain that she didn't reciprocate it. And having to face once and for all the fact that he had feelings for Rosemary March that she didn't and wouldn't return was something he just couldn't afford to have interfering with his studies.

His studies. Yeah, that was it. He was hip-deep in a very important research project that required a lot of cerebral exercise. He couldn't afford to be distracted by other, more emotional, pursuits right now. Especially emotional pursuits that threatened to consume him whole if he even came close to attempting to analyze them.

"The things I said to you last night were completely uncalled for," he told Rosemary softly, deliberately avoiding any mention of his past transgressions. "And I apologize for saying them."

She nodded, obviously understanding that he wasn't going to offer her any more than that. "Okay," she said simply.

Although he hated to prolong the scene, he needed to know for sure that they were square on the matter. "So you forgive me?" he asked through gritted teeth.

She nodded. "I forgive you for saying the things you said to me last night."

It was as good as he was going to get, he knew. Which was just as well, seeing as how he was in no way interested in exploring their past any more than they already had. He had a comet to nail down before he could address any other aspect of his life.

"Fine," he muttered.

"Fine," she echoed.

"As long as that's settled."

"That's settled."

So everything was settled, he told himself. Then why was he still hanging around? "Do you want to see the comet?" he asked impulsively, surprising himself.

She, too, was clearly surprised by his offer, because she arched her eyebrows inquisitively. Then her eyes cleared of the clouds that had been present in them since she'd awakened to find him touching her hand. "Bob? Really?" she asked, her tone of voice indicating how much she'd love to take him up on the offer.

Willis bit back a retort at the layman's term for Bobrzyny-ckolonycki and nodded. "It will be visible to the naked eye by tomorrow night, but if you'd like to get a look close up, through the telescope, you're welcome to."

She smiled a small smile, and something inside Willis turned over at the sight. She really was interested in his work, he thought. Even if she didn't have a hope in hell of ever understanding what he did for a living, the idea of the comet thrilled her almost as much as it did him.

But for entirely different reasons, naturally, he knew. Where he was fascinated by Bobrzynyckolonycki's inexplicable be-havior as it sped through the cosmos, Rosemary, like every other member of the general public, obviously just found the idea of a comet to be—to put it in layman's terms—really, really neato.

"Come on up," he said, gesturing over his shoulder toward the stairs. "I promise you you'll never see anything like it again. Not for another fifteen years, anyway," he added with a smile.

It was a peace offering, and Willis held his breath as he waited to see if she would accept it. He knew she had when she smiled at him. It wasn't a big smile, but it wasn't bad. It was certainly better than the hurt expression she had been wearing.

"Okay," she said. "I'd love to see Bob up close and per-sonal."

"Then come on."

She hesitated only a moment before setting the throw pillow aside and rising from the couch. Thankfully, her nightshirt dropped down to just below her knees, but those sexy calves still mocked him. Spinning quickly around, Willis headed back toward the stairs, trusting that Rosemary would follow him. No way was he going to risk another glance at those legs.

His Mussorgsky CD had segued to *A Night on Bald Mountain* by the time they scaled the attic steps, and he could see that Rosemary was startled by his choice in music—not to mention his choice in volume.

"Wow," she said. "Don't you find it difficult to concentrate with all that going on?"

He shook his head. "Actually, I find it difficult to concentrate without it. I like the roar of chaos surrounding me when I'm studying the universe. It just seems appropriate somehow."

Rosemary told him, "I like listening to songs like 'Gangsters' by The Specials or 'House of Fun' by Madness when I'm working. You know, songs with a good beat that are easy to dance to."

Willis bit his lip to keep in the cutting remark that tried to escape from his mouth. Instead, he asked, "Travel agents do a lot of dancing while they work, do they?"

She smiled. "Only when their bosses are out of the office."

He sat down on the stool beside the telescope and peered into the eyepiece to position the instrument so that Rosemary would have the best view. Assuring himself he was only asking to make conversation, he inquired further, "What made you decide to become a travel agent?"

He was still gazing into the telescope, so he couldn't see her face when she answered, but something in her voice troubled him.

"I always wanted to travel," she said. "I thought being a travel agent would give me an opportunity to do that."

When he turned his attention to her, he found her studying her hands a little nervously. "But your mother said you suffer from motion sickness, a fear of flying, claustrophob—"

"Yeah, I do," she said, interrupting his litany of her various shortcomings. "But I didn't realize that until *after* I became a travel agent. By trying to travel. By then, it was too late. I wasn't trained to do anything else." She lifted her chin a defensive inch or two, but still didn't quite meet his gaze. "Besides, I like what I do, and I'm good at it. Even if I can't travel myself."

Willis knew better than to challenge her, simply because he knew they'd both jump at the chance to bicker. And he didn't doubt for a moment that she was good at her job. Even if it did involve the use of computers.

"So you're a travel agent who sticks close to home, is that it?" he asked.

She nodded, then finally flickered her gaze anxiously up to his. "Yeah. Is that such a bad thing?"

He shook his head. "No. I just wonder sometimes if you still think about visiting other places."

Like Boston.

The thought erupted in his brain without warning, and he immediately shoved it aside. Just what he needed. Rosemary coming to Boston and turning his world upside down. He could already see the expressions on his colleagues' faces when he introduced her. Their mouths would drop open in undisguised lust at the sight of her. Then she'd open *her* mouth and ask something about kumquat physics, and they'd turn their dumbfounded gazes to Willis, silently wondering if he'd lost his brilliant mind.

"I like Endicott just fine," she told him, though something in her voice contradicted her assurance. "It's my home. It's where my friends and family are. Why would I want to go anywhere else?"

He lifted a shoulder and let it drop. "I don't know. But there are a lot of interesting places out there to visit." And then, even though he'd forbidden himself to so much as consider the concept, he heard himself blurt out, "Boston, for example, has enough going on at any given moment to keep you fascinated for a lifetime."

She narrowed her eyes at him. "That almost sounds like an invitation," she said carefully.

Willis felt himself coloring. "It *wasn't* an invitation," he said, feeling it important to make that perfectly clear.

She eyed him thoughtfully. "Okay, it wasn't an invitation. I appreciate the offer."

"It wasn't an offer, either," he told her hastily.

This time Willis was the one to narrow his eyes. Hadn't they had this conversation once before? When Rosemary had issued her noninvitation-nonoffer for him to join her for dinner? And hadn't she turned around and acted offended that he hadn't taken her up on it? Surely he wasn't going to—

"Okay," she said, interrupting his ruminations. "It wasn't an offer, either. It doesn't matter, anyway, because I don't want to go to Boston. I don't want to go anywhere. I want to stay in Endicott for the rest of my life, okay?"

Funny, she didn't sound okay. She sounded anguished. Uncertain. Annoyed. Then again, she was talking to him, right? Of course she'd be annoyed.

He jerked his gaze away from her and looked through the eyepiece of his telescope again. "Fine. You want to live and die in Endicott. Sounds like a fitting end."

"What's that supposed to mean?"

He sighed heavily as he brought the comet into focus. "Nothing, Rosemary. It doesn't mean anything."

Actually, that wasn't true, he knew. It did mean something. It meant that Rosemary March fit into the southern Indiana landscape perfectly. The lush, rolling hillsides and clear blue skies and easy, languid pace of life fit her exactly. In a lot of ways, she belonged here. Just like the rest of Willis's past. And when the Comet Festival was over, he could leave her behind, along with all his other memories.

He tried not to dwell on the fact that although he'd been absent from Endicott for thirteen years, and although many of his memories of his hometown had indeed faded, there was one that had remained crystal clear for more than a decade, one that had followed him to Cambridge, one that still crept out of the corners of his mind from time to time, just to drive him crazy.

It was the vision of Rosemary March leaving their high-school graduation on the arm of Walt Zapfel, the pitcher for the Endicott Central Yellowjackets baseball team. She'd been gazing over her shoulder at Willis, holding her gold mortarboard down on her dark curls. The wind had whipped up around the gold graduation gown she hadn't bothered to zip, churning her flowered skirt above her knees.

And she'd smiled at him.

Actually smiled. Not the tight, thin, sarcastic smile she usually tossed at him when she cut him to the quick, but a warm, wistful smile that had grabbed hold of his heart with both fists and sent his pulse skyrocketing. A smile that had seemed to him then…affectionate. A smile that had made him feel as though she was genuinely going to miss him when they went their separate ways. And then Walt had slung his arm around her shoulders and pulled her close, and Rosemary had turned away.

Willis had tucked that smile into the dark recesses of his mind, thinking it would eventually dissolve and not bother him again. But he'd been wrong. That smile had crept out of the darkness again and again over the years, only to plague him with confusion.

That memory, like all his others from high school, belonged right here in Endicott, he told himself now. Not in Cambridge, where he had created an entirely new life, a life that was as far removed from the pizza-faced little twerp he'd been before as Bobrzynyckolonycki was removed from the earth.

But if that was true, he mused further, then why did he keep wondering what Rosemary would look like, warm and pink and naked—and smiling at him affectionately as she had on the day of their graduation—from the side of his bed back in Cambridge that was always empty and cold?

Six

Rosemary watched as Willis rose from the stool beside his telescope, and wondered what she had done this time to make him frown. But before she could ask, he stepped away and gestured silently toward the seat he had just vacated. Eyeing him cautiously, still not certain what exactly had made him mad, she perched herself on the stool. Then, gingerly, more than a little fearful that she would break the big machine just by touching it, she gripped the eyepiece and bent her head toward it.

Immediately, her posture changed. Where before she had been rigid and defensive, suddenly she slumped her shoulders forward and dropped her mouth open. "Oh, Willis," she whispered. "That's amazing. That's Bob?"

"That's Bobrzynyckolonycki," he told her, his voice rough, quiet.

"It's...it's..." She drew in a deep breath and held it for long moments, but didn't utter a sound beyond that.

"It's beautiful, isn't it?" he asked her.

All she could do was nod, awed by the sight that greeted

her. Bob was indeed beautiful. A spray of translucent white and blue against an ebony backdrop spattered with stars, like diamonds cast down on black velvet. The comet appeared to be transfixed in space, millions of miles beyond her grasp, yet seemingly close enough to reach out and touch.

Rosemary smiled as she continued to observe what before had been nothing more to her than a minuscule dot of light in the sky. "No wonder you've always been so fascinated by this stuff," she said softly.

She felt him draw nearer behind her. "Here," he said, reaching forward. "Let me show you this 'stuff,' as you call it, from another angle."

As she pulled away from the eyepiece, he bent toward the telescope—which naturally necessitated bending toward Rosemary, too—and touched one of the larger knobs at the base to turn the scope slightly. Then he bent even closer to her, gazing through the eyepiece, scarcely an inch away from her, and adjusted another knob, explaining quietly that it would sharpen the focus.

As he did so, she was assaulted by his scent, something earthy and musky and masculine. His heat wrapped around her, enveloping her, and she felt as if she were almost becoming one with him. His shoulder brushed softly against hers, and although both of them froze at the contact, neither of them moved to end it.

For one long moment, Willis stood close enough for her to rope both arms around him and pull him close, and bury her face in his neck and chest, and cover his mouth with hers. If, of course, that was what she wanted to do. And God help her, she suddenly realized, for some reason, that was exactly what she wanted to do.

When she felt herself starting to sway toward him, she swallowed hard and reminded herself of the disdain that had dripped from his voice when he'd repeated her word for his interests and occupation—*stuff*. And with the reminder that he held so much contempt for her lack of knowledge, she finally found the power to launch her emotional retro-rockets and pull out of his orbit.

An Important Message from the Editors of Silhouette®

Dear Reader,

Because you've chosen to read one of our fine romance novels, we'd like to say "thank you!" And, as a <u>special</u> way to thank you, we've selected <u>two more</u> of the books you love so well, <u>plus</u> an exciting mystery gift, to send you absolutely **FREE!**

Please enjoy them with our compliments...

Candy Lee

Editor

P.S. And because we <u>*value*</u> *our customers, we've attached something extra inside...*

Peel off seal and place inside...

How to validate your
Editor's FREE GIFT "Thank You"

1. Peel off gift seal from front cover. Place it in space provided at right. This automatically entitles you to receive two free books and a fabulous mystery gift.

2. Send back this card and you'll get brand-new Silhouette Desire® novels. These books have a cover price of $3.75 each, but they are yours to keep absolutely free.

3. There's no catch. You're under no obligation to buy anything. We charge nothing—ZERO—for your first shipment. And you don't have to make any minimum number of purchases—not even one!

4. The fact is thousands of readers enjoy receiving books by mail from the Silhouette Reader Service™. They like the convenience of home delivery...they like getting the best new novels BEFORE they're available in stores... and they love our discount prices!

5. We hope that after receiving your free books you'll want to remain a subscriber. But the choice is yours— to continue or cancel, any time at all! So why not take us up on our invitation, with no risk of any kind. You'll be glad you did!

6. Don't forget to detach your FREE BOOKMARK. And remember...just for validating your Editor's Free Gift Offer, we'll send you THREE gifts, *ABSOLUTELY FREE!*

GET A **FREE** MYSTERY GIFT...

YOURS FREE!

*SURPRISE MYSTERY GIFT COULD BE YOURS **FREE** AS A SPECIAL "THANK YOU" FROM THE EDITORS OF SILHOUETTE*

So what if she didn't know the proper terminology for his studies? she thought. What was so terrible about that? Why couldn't she just enjoy the view of the cosmos for what it was—a vista of nature and beauty that defied explanation or control? She didn't have to understand the workings of the universe to be awed by it. On the contrary, she could probably appreciate the spectacle more than Willis could, precisely because she *wasn't* trying to pin it down.

Maybe it was better not to overanalyze some things, she thought. Like the universe, for example. Or her feelings for Willis Random.

He stepped away from the telescope and again gestured silently that she should look through the eyepiece. When she did, she saw that the comet's tail was more evident now, two long shafts of nearly transparent blue and yellowish white. She shook her head in marvel at the sight.

"What exactly is a comet, anyway?" she asked. As an afterthought, telling herself she was *not* doing it to bait him, she added, "In terms that we lowly members of the *laity* might understand, I mean. I don't want to get brain strain, after all, do I?"

He sighed fitfully, but offered no other indication that he had detected her sarcasm. "It's a great big hunk of ice and dirt, speeding through the cosmos," he told her.

"How can a hunk of ice burn?" she asked.

"It's not actually burning," he said. "It's glowing."

Still gazing through the eyepiece, she asked him, "Okay, then how can a hunk of ice glow?"

He sighed again, and this time she thought it was probably because he didn't want to have to explain something so complicated as dirt and ice speeding through the cosmos to someone like her, who couldn't possibly understand such a thing with such a tiny brain.

"Never mind," she told him shortly, pulling her head back from the eyepiece to look at him, instead. "Forget I even asked."

"Rosemary—"

He uttered her name impatiently, as if he wanted to say

more, but wasn't sure what. For a long moment, he only gazed at her, then he pulled up the chair by his desk and seated himself beside her.

"The nucleus of a comet," he began, "that's the center part, is a solid mass of ice and debris. As the comet moves through the solar system toward the sun, the sun warms it, and the icy surface turns immediately to gas. Then sunlight excites the gas, making it glow with a faint, bluish light. The gas rushing away from the sun makes one part of the comet's tail. The other part of the tail is made of dust particles, which fan out along the comet's orbit and reflect the sunlight."

She smiled at him and tried not to sound too brittle as she said, "See? That wasn't so hard, was it? I understood everything you said. Guess I'm not as dumb as I look, huh?"

"Rosemary," he said again. Yet once more, he halted at her name, as if he wasn't sure what else to say.

"What?" she asked.

But he only continued to study her in silence.

"Willis, please," she said softly. "If you have something to say to me, just say it. Don't sit there and look at me like I'm some repugnant little germ under a microscope that you're trying to find a cure for."

He arched his eyebrows at that. "Was I looking at you that way?"

She nodded and dropped her gaze to the floor. "Yes."

"I apologize then. I don't want to make you feel like a repugnant little germ."

No, just a simpleminded, slack-brained know-nothing, she thought. *That's all.*

"Thanks for showing me Bob," she muttered as she rose from the stool. "It was nice of you."

"Wait, don't leave," he said, and she was sure she must have imagined the note of panic that punctuated his words. "There's a lot more than Bobrzynyckolonycki up there that I could show you. If you want, I mean…"

His voice trailed off, and something in his tone urged her not to be so hasty to leave. Well, that and the small, almost hopeful-looking smile playing about his lips.

"Like what?" she asked as she sat back down again, feeling a little wary nonetheless.

"Like…like Magellanic Clouds, for instance."

"Magellanic Clouds?" she repeated. The first word felt uncomfortable on her tongue, yet for some reason, it generated an odd kind of warmth deep inside her.

He nodded. "And globular clusters, nebulae, quasars, stars."

As he spoke so easily and eloquently of the mysteries of the universe, the warmth that had blossomed deep inside Rosemary began to spread outward, gradually heating her belly and her chest. "Stars?" she asked, seizing on the only part of his statement that she recognized. She hoped she only imagined the breathlessness that seemed to surround that single word. "What kind of stars?"

He seemed to be studying her with a strange expression on his face, as if he suddenly wasn't quite sure what to make of her. But he said nothing in response to her question.

"Tell me," she demanded. "What kind of stars? Name some for me, Willis."

"Okay," he replied. But something in his voice sounded a bit strained. "Like…like Beta Pictoris, for example," he told her. "Or…or Regulus. Aldebaran, Arcturus, Procyon, Rasalhague…."

The heat inside Rosemary began to churn as he rattled off the unfamiliar words, until it swirled into a seething mass of turmoil, spilling into her heart, her hands, her head. And suddenly, with the force of a meteor crashing into the earth, she remembered something that she had all but forgotten. She remembered that she had always been completely turned on—yes, by Willis Random—whenever he started talking like a scientist.

Oh, God. How could she have forgotten about that?

It had been the bane of her adolescent years, her guilty pleasure, her embarrassing desire. As much as she had loathed Willis, as awful as he'd made her feel at times, she'd been completely overwhelmed sexually by his big brain. Intelligence, as far as Rosemary had always been concerned, was just *soooo* sexy. Even when she was only fifteen, she had always become utterly aroused by intellectual talk. Mathematical talk. Philosophical talk. Scientific talk.

And Willis had offered more than his fair share of those. Forget big biceps and broad shoulders. What had turned Rosemary on as a teenager—and what evidently still turned her on to this day—had been big brains and broad IQs.

Suddenly, she understood why she'd had so few fulfilling relationships as an adult woman—because she never went out with particularly intelligent men. There simply were no chemists or physicists, no mathematicians or statisticians, no economic or computer whizzes anywhere in town. And evidently, those were the kind of men Rosemary was destined to need. To want. To lust after.

Back in high school, the story had been the same. Although she'd dated the athletes and popular boys at Endicott Central—because they'd been the ones to ask her out—she'd been far more interested in boys who could do things like recite the periodic table from memory. Boys who could explain with ease the molecular structure of H_2SO_4. Boys who could split atoms in their basements after dinner. That kind of thing. And there had only been one boy at Endicott Central who could do all that.

Willis Random.

Kirby and Angie were right—there *had* been more to the antagonism she'd always felt for Willis than a simple adolescent contempt for a geek who drove her crazy. On the contrary, Rosemary had always had a full-blown crush on the geek, and simply hadn't wanted to admit it, not even to herself. A full-blown crush on a pizza-faced little twerp who thought she was just about the dumbest person to ever walk the earth.

Back in high school, she'd actually been infatuated with Willis's big brain and even bigger IQ. More accurately, she'd actually been infatuated with Willis. And that was why she'd fought so bitterly against him—because she hadn't wanted anyone to find out.

What a stupid girl she'd been after all.

And now, here was Willis, looking like a Greek god, talking

scientific to her all over again, when her needs, wants and lusts had matured as much as the rest of her had. It was almost more than she could bear.

"Oh, Willis," she whispered.

She told herself to flee now while she still had some semblance of dignity left. She screamed to her brain to get her body out of there before she did something utterly humiliating that she'd never be able to live down. She begged with what little sanity she had left to please, please rescue her from her weakness.

But what she said out loud was, "Please, Willis...tell me *more*."

Funny how he seemed to be suddenly zooming his focus on her face, she thought. He looked as if he were actually interested in what he saw there. Then he narrowed his eyes at her.

"Rosemary?" he asked, his voice indicating clearly his concern for her welfare.

"Hmm?" she purred.

"Are you okay?"

"Oh, I'm fine. Just fine." Her words sounded too slow, too sultry, and she tried to force a more level timbre as she added, "I just want to hear more about the universe. Tell me *more*, Willis, please," she pleaded, her voice sounding husky and not at all normal. "*Please* tell me more."

"Well...okay," he said, though he was obviously not convinced of her...fineness. He watched her cautiously as he told her, "There are also moons we could see pretty well from here."

She nodded. Moons. Oh, yeah. That sounded great. "Like what?" she asked.

"Like...Titan, Rhea, Iapetus, Dione and Tethys...those are Saturn's moons."

She licked her lips against the dryness that was overtaking her throat and mouth and swiped a hand over the perspiration forming on her forehead. "What else?"

He continued to study her warily. "Uh...galaxies."

"Such as?"

He hesitated a moment, as if he wasn't sure whether or not she was serious. Then he began softly, "Well, there's Andromeda, M87, M33, NGC 5128, the Coma cluster...."

"Oh, yeah," she said with a slow nod. "That's good. That's real good. What else?"

He cleared his throat a little uncomfortably. "Well, I suppose if you really want to get into it, we could talk about gravitational pull or centrifugal force." He shrugged, but there was nothing careless about the gesture. "Rotational dynamics, even—torque and angular acceleration, that kind of thing."

She tugged at the neck of her nightshirt, whose damp fabric had begun to cling to her chest. Then she closed her eyes and murmured, "Oooh, yesss. More, Willis. *More.*"

When he didn't say anything else, she opened her eyes again, only to find that he had leaned forward a little, close enough for her to inhale the rich, musky, male scent of him again. Helplessly, she felt herself swaying toward him.

He took off his glasses, as if he were having trouble distinguishing her features at such close range, then began to rapidly wipe the lenses with the hem of his T-shirt. But his gaze never left hers. "Say, Rosemary, are you sure you're, um...okay?"

She nodded quickly and leaned a bit more toward him. "Oh...oh, yes, Willis...I'm fine...." She covered his hand with hers, and he immediately stopped cleaning his glasses. "What else?" she whispered. "Tell me more about the universe. I want *more.*"

"O-okay," he stammered, his expression changing to one of extreme discomfort. Without removing her hand from his, he folded the earpieces down on his glasses and set them on his desk. "Um, well...perhaps we'd better just stick to the basics for now. The planets, for example. Saturn's rings alone can make for fascinating discussion. And let's not forget Jupiter's Great Red Spot..."

"Oh, no," she murmured, lifting her other hand to his hair, threading her fingers through the soft, silky tresses before she could stop herself. "Let's not forget that Great...Red...Spot...."

Talk of telescopes and Great Red Spots was the last straw,

and slowly, so slowly, Rosemary curved her palm over the back of his head and gently urged him toward her. "Oh, Willis..." she whispered before she could stop herself.

He allowed her to pull him closer, even lifted his hand to her hair, too, touching his fingertip to the damp, wayward curl that had plastered itself to her cheek. His voice was almost inaudible when he asked her, "Yes, Rosemary?"

"Would you be offended if I asked you to..."

"To what?"

"To...kiss me?"

Instead of waiting for him to act on her request, she tightened her grip on the back of his head and pulled him toward her, covering his mouth with hers before he had a chance to say no.

Not that she got the impression that he was going to say no. In fact, the moment her lips touched his, he roped both arms around her waist and jerked her quickly toward him, until her breasts were crushed against that hard, massive, magnificent chest, and she could feel his heart pounding against her own, every bit as rapidly and raggedly as hers was.

Willis wanted her. He really wanted her. Somehow the vague realization of that penetrated her brain through the fog of need and wanting that had set her aflame. His response to her embrace was every bit as immediate and intense as her desire for him was. He was kissing her back without qualm or inhibition.

And boy, was he a good kisser.

When she buried both hands in his hair and slanted her mouth over his, he lifted her from her seat to pull her into his lap. Over and over again, he kissed her, first roughly, then gently, then quickly, then slowly, as if he had no idea just how he wanted to handle her. She fidgeted in his lap and felt him ripen hard and fast against her fanny, and she dropped her head backward to utter a soft moan.

Willis took advantage of her position to drag his open mouth down along the damp skin of her neck, rubbing his hot, hungry lips over the column of her throat. The hand at her waist dropped to the hem of her nightshirt, then he began to push the fabric higher, higher, higher, until he was cupping her upper thigh in eager fingers. He brought his mouth back to hers, then moved his hand higher still, until he cradled one soft globe of her derriere in his palm.

"Oh," Rosemary murmured. "Oh, Willis…"

With a gasp, he captured his name from her mouth, then thrust his tongue inside to taste her deeply. Deliberately, she ground her hips against his lap, twisting and turning in an effort to straddle him. He seemed to sense her intentions, because he shifted, too, adjusting both their bodies to the position she craved. When she sat in his lap facing him, her legs dangling over each of his, he dropped both hands to her fanny, and shoved her nightshirt higher, until it was bunched around her waist.

Then higher still, dragging his fingertips over her ribs, curling the fingers of each hand under her breasts. Rosemary's breath caught in her throat at the intimate touch, but she neither said nor did anything to stop his exploration. Willis, however, hesitated for a moment, and she nearly panicked, fearing his withdrawal. So she closed one of her hands over his and urged it higher, cupping his warm, rough fingers over the soft, heated flesh of her breast.

"Oh, Rosemary…" he whispered, his voice softening when he uttered her name, as if it were a benediction.

She closed her fingers over his, both of them squeezing her tender flesh, until he found the stiff peak and caught it between thumb and forefinger. For a moment, he rolled her nipple gently, then he dipped his head toward her and drew her full into his mouth.

The damp heat of his tongue assaulted her, and Rosemary closed her eyes to enjoy the sensations. Hungrily, he devoured her, his breathing ragged and loud, his mouth wreaking havoc like none she'd ever experienced before. She furrowed her fingers through his hair and held his head in place, worried that he would soon come to his senses and push her away, worried more that he wouldn't and that things would go too far.

But strangely, that was exactly what she wanted. To go too

far. With Willis. For one brief, anxious moment, she wondered how things between them had changed so quickly, so completely. Then he turned his attentions to her other breast, and as he suckled her gently, then roughly, she ceased to think at all.

When he finally pulled back to gaze upon her face, he covered both breasts with his big hands and closed his fingers possessively over her. She dipped her head toward his, furrowed her fingers more desperately through his hair and kissed him again. For long moments, their lips and tongues warred over possession, then Rosemary curled the fingers of both hands around his nape and sought another plan of action. Instinctively, intuitively, she urged her hips forward, thrusting the heated, damp core of herself against the solid ridge that strained against the fabric of his shorts.

This time Willis was the one to lean his head back on a groan, and Rosemary dipped her own head to taste the rough, salty skin of his neck. She traced the tip of her tongue along his warm flesh, nibbling at the hollow at the base of his throat before circling it with her tongue again. The hands covering her breasts clenched tighter, and again she rubbed herself sinuously, shamelessly, against him.

Willis froze at the contact, and for a moment, Rosemary feared she had gone too far. She, too, stilled, waiting to see what he would do. Slowly, the hands cupping her breasts relaxed, and she closed her eyes against the rejection she felt coming. Then he lowered his hands to cup her fanny and squeezed her tender flesh with eager fingers, silently urging her forward.

"Again," he said softly, raggedly.

She opened her eyes and met his gaze levelly as she thrust her hips forward, emitting a small, helpless sound at the dizzying ripple of delight that wound through her.

He sucked in a rough breath and exhaled raggedly, but his eyes never left hers. "Again," he told her.

Once more, she bucked softly against him, biting back a gasp of ecstasy.

He shook his head almost imperceptibly, then neared her

again, softly nuzzling the line of her jaw with his warm rough cheek. So quietly, she almost didn't hear him, he murmured, "Again, Rosemary. Again."

This time she dropped her hands to his shoulders and, gripping his hard muscles fiercely, rocked her hips back and forth, slowly, deliberately, riding astride him. For long moments, she moved forward, then backward, then forward again, quickening the pace, then slowing it, until the friction of their clothes against their sensitive flesh nearly drove them both over the edge.

This time Willis was the one to close his eyes, and he dropped his head backward again. "Ah, Rosemary..." he began, his voice trailing off.

She didn't like the way he uttered her name, so helplessly, so anxiously, so completely without hope. Reluctantly, she ceased her movements atop him. Without opening his eyes, he removed his hands from her fanny and lifted them to her waist. Silently, she bade him to skim his fingers higher, to go back and make the top part of her body feel as wobbly as the bottom part did. And for one brief moment, she was certain that was what he was going to do.

Then slowly, and with obvious reluctance, he reached for her nightshirt and pushed it back down around her hips as well as he could. Then he gripped her waist again—this time with surer fingers—effortlessly lifted her from his lap, and deposited her onto her feet beside him.

But he didn't let her go.

Instead, still holding her waist, he bent forward, until his forehead was pressed gently against her belly. Rosemary threaded her fingers gingerly through his hair and willed herself not to fall apart.

At her gentle caress, he stirred, then slowly, he straightened and released her. He rose awkwardly from his chair and turned his back to her, staring out the open attic window at the limitless black sky beyond.

"That," he said softly, "was a very big mistake."

Rosemary swallowed hard against the lump that swelled in her throat. "Why?" she asked, the single word resounding hollowly off the bare, honey-colored beams of the walls and ceiling enclosing them.

"Because..." he said. But his voice trailed off before he offered her an adequate answer.

She took a few tentative steps forward and placed her open palm at the center of his back. Immediately, he spun around and away from her. "Don't," he said, holding his own hand, palm out, toward her.

"Willis..." she began as she took a step toward him, hating the pleading in her voice that punctuated his name. "What's wrong?"

He shook his head slowly and took a step backward to compensate for the one she had taken forward. And with that one tiny gesture, what little hope Rosemary had tried to hold on to evaporated. She met his gaze levelly, but had no idea what to say.

Which was just as well, because evidently Willis had something he wanted to ask her himself. "What the hell brought that on?" he said, his voice rough, almost angry sounding.

Excellent question, Rosemary thought. She lifted one shoulder and let it drop. "I don't know," she said honestly. "Just, when you started saying all that stuff...when you started talking all scientific like that, I...I..."

He hesitated only a moment before asking, "You what?"

"I just..." But still she left unfinished whatever it was she was going to say, and instead only gazed at him with helpless hunger.

"You just what?" Willis demanded.

"I just got..." She shook her head silently, not sure how to reveal her feelings.

"You just got *what?*" His expression was frantic somehow, almost as if he didn't want to hear what she had to say, despite his insistence that she enlighten him. "Dammit, Rosemary," he said adamantly, "tell me. You just got *what?*"

"I just got *soooo...*"

"What, Rosemary, what? For God's sake, you just got so *what?*"

She shrugged helplessly. "I just got so...*turned on.*"

"You what?"

She stared at him helplessly. "I got turned on," she repeated. "By you. You may not realize this, Willis, but you're really sexy. I just wanted…"

She bit off her words before she could say any more, embarrassed by how much she had revealed already. She wondered what he would say if she confessed that she had always felt that way about him, that even when he was a pizza-faced little twerp of thirteen, she'd had a raging crush on him the size of Jupiter's Great Red Spot. That all through high school, even when he was no longer her chemistry partner, even when he had made clear his disdain for her appalling lack of gray matter, she'd carried a torch for him bright enough to dim the most powerful supernova.

That the reason she was still a single woman to this day was that she'd never quite gotten over him.

She opened her mouth, ready to bare her soul and put voice to exactly those thoughts, helpless to stop herself from spilling her guts all over the floor, right at his feet, regardless of the consequences. But something in his expression cut her off, quickly and unequivocally prohibiting her from telling him what she so badly wanted to tell him.

Willis stared at her silently for a long moment, as if he had no idea what language she was even speaking. Then a muscle in his cheek twitched, and he chuckled—a solitary expulsion of air completely lacking in humor. And then he said softly, evenly, "But that's ridiculous, Rosemary. Not only was none of what I said even remotely suggestive, but you couldn't possibly have understood or appreciated a word of it."

She snapped her mouth shut and felt heat seep into her face, and wished she would just drop through the attic floor. And then through the second floor, and then the first floor, and then the basement, and then the earth's crust. Because she suddenly felt the urge to flee to the very center of the planet, where the heat of the earth's core might potentially burn away her stupid, *stupid* feelings for Willis Random.

As if he hadn't already said enough, he added, "I mean, things like globular clusters and rotational acceleration aren't *too* very difficult for *most* people to fathom, but *you*, Rosemary..." He moved quickly back to his desk, reached for his glasses and hastily unfolded them to settle them back on his face. "There's no way *you* could ever..."

She held up a hand to stop the onslaught of insult and bit out, "I get the picture, Willis. You don't have to say any more."

She turned her back on him, then with all the dignity she could muster—which, frankly, wasn't much dignity at all— she strode as quickly as she could toward the hole in the attic floor that promised escape and sanctuary.

"Wait, Rosemary," he called after her. "I didn't mean to imply that you were..." His voice halted before he finished what he was going to say.

She spun back around, blinking against the heavy moisture that pooled in her eyes. "Oh, yes, you did," she countered, nearly choking on the words. "The term you can't seem to say, Willis, is 'stupid.' And you most definitely meant to imply that I'm exactly that. Stupid."

"No, Rosemary, I assure you—"

"Go to hell," she snarled. "You thought I was stupid when we were in school, and you think I'm stupid now. You'll always think I'm stupid, no matter what I say or do. So just...go to hell," she repeated on a sob.

Then, before she *really* embarrassed herself by crying, Rosemary bolted down the attic stairs and into her bedroom, leaped up into her bed and pulled the covers up over her head.

She wasn't stupid. She wasn't. But where Willis Random was concerned, she would always have the brain capacity of a slug. Damn him. Then again, she thought morosely, if falling in love with such a man didn't qualify her for the post of Queen Stupid, she didn't know what would.

Maybe Willis was right after all, she thought. Because even though he carried a low opinion of her intelligence, she still felt herself falling in love with him. Just like the simple-minded, slack-brained, know-nothing girl in high school had.

Rosemary curled up into a tight, tiny ball, then buried her face in her pillow and began to cry. Stupid, stupid, stupid, she thought, the litany so very appropriate. *Stupid, stupid, stupid…*

Seven

She managed to avoid Willis for a full thirty-seven hours, forty-two minutes and eighteen seconds before she encountered him again. And then she acknowledged him only because he trapped her in her bedroom. As she dressed for her friend Angie's wedding—Angie's *wedding,* for God's sake—he rapped on her bedroom door softly.

"Rosemary?" he called quietly from the other side.

For a long moment, she tried to ignore him, telling herself that if she didn't say anything to him, ever again, for the rest of her life, maybe she could forget he had ever existed in the first place. Then a memory of that damned kissing and groping they'd enjoyed in the attic two nights before flared to life in her brain, and she realized she would never be able to forget Willis Random in any way, shape or form.

"Rosemary," he called out again when she didn't answer, a bit more loudly this time.

"What?" she snapped.

"I need to talk to you."

"About what?"

She half expected him to say something like she was out of coffee, or that he needed more batteries for his calculator or that her car was due for its fifty-thousand-mile oil change or something.

So it came as a pretty major surprise when he said quietly through the door, "About us."

She swallowed hard and looked at her reflection in the dresser mirror, hating the hopeful little glimmer she saw in her expression. Even worse was the rosy glow that warmed her entire body at the prospect of seeing him again. And because she was standing there in her underwear—pink underwear, at that—she could see that that glow covered every inch of skin revealed.

You sucker, she berated herself. She was *not* going to fall for this. No matter what he had to say, no matter how much he tried to apologize for what had happened the other night, she was *not* going to forgive him this time.

And she wasn't going to gaze into those midnight-blue eyes of his and turn into Jell-O, either. Nor was she going to succumb to the whimpering desire that sputtered to life in her midsection every time she got within two feet of him. And she most definitely would not grow warm at the sound of her name on those finely chiseled lips.

"There's nothing to talk about," she called toward her bedroom door. "Go away."

"I think there's plenty to talk about," he countered. "And I'm not going away until we talk about it."

"Thanks very much, Willis, but I think you've insulted me enough for one lifetime. I'm not going to listen to anything you have to say anymore. *Go...away.*"

"I'm sorry."

His voice softened as he uttered his apology, and she felt her resolve begin to crumble. So she rallied it as best she could and told him, "Not good enough."

"Rosemary, please. Talk to me. Just give me a chance to explain."

"Explain what? Why you can't let bygones be bygones? Why you can't accept an apology from a woman for things

she said when she was a teenager, for God's sake? Or is it
that you want to explain why you can't make love to a woman
whose IQ is lower than yours?''

''No,'' he replied curtly. ''What I want to explain is why I
can't allow myself to be distracted by a beautiful woman when
I have such important work to do.''

Rosemary spun around and eyed her bedroom door suspiciously. Beautiful? Willis was calling her *beautiful?* Slowly,
she crossed her bedroom to the door and placed her open palm
gingerly against it.

''You think I'm beautiful?'' she asked, hating herself for
needing confirmation from the likes of him.

For a moment, he said nothing. Then she heard a heavy
sigh, followed by a quietly uttered, ''Yes. I do.''

Oh, great, Rosemary thought. Willis had actually paid her
a compliment. Now what was she supposed to do? She nibbled
her lip thoughtfully, then pushed herself away from the door.
Maybe she was being a bit rash in her haste to condemn Willis.
Maybe she should listen to what he had to say. Hey, what was
so terrible about giving him another chance, right? What did
she have to lose? Maybe he would even tell her she was beautiful again.

You sucker, she chastised herself immediately again. *What
do you have to lose? How about what little self-respect you
have left?*

''Wait a minute,'' she told him, assuring herself she only
imagined the shiver in her voice when she spoke. ''I'm getting
dressed. I'll be out in a minute.''

He said nothing more, but she heard him move away from
the door. She crossed quickly to her closet, yanked out a pale-
yellow sleeveless linen sheath and jerked it over her head. Her
fingers shook as she fumbled with the big white buttons that
closed it from scooped neck to just above her knees, so she
forced herself to stop and take a deep breath.

It was only Willis, she reminded herself. A guy she'd
known for half her life, a guy she had at one time been able
to pick up and toss into a swimming pool. Why was she so
intimidated by him? Just because now he was gorgeous and

sexy and weighed twice as much as she did? Just because his IQ was probably twice her own, as well? Just because he was a fantastic kisser who tied her libido in knots? Just because he had pushed her away in a fit of disgust at the height of her desire?

Hey, what was there to be intimidated about? Sheesh.

The mid-September day was warm, so she didn't bother with panty hose, and instead slid her bare feet into flat pumps the same buttery color as her dress. After fastening small gold hoops in her ears, hooking a thin gold chain around her neck and sliding a half-dozen gold bangles over one wrist, she sprayed herself lightly with perfume and ran a brush through her brief, unruly curls.

There, she thought as she turned first one way and then the other in front of her mirror. She looked pretty intelligent dressed this way, if she said so herself.

Downstairs, Willis was pacing the length of the living room as Ska and Isosceles sat side by side on the window seat, looking like matching salt and pepper shakers, watching him. He shook his head in amazement at the animals—one bright white and one a mixture of darks, one triangular and one rather oval—neither having the slightest trait in common. One day, the two cats had been at each other's throats, and the next, they were curled up beside each other as if they'd been best buddies for life.

Cats, he thought dismally. And here they were reputed to be such intelligent creatures.

A sound on the stairs caught his attention, and he spun around to find Rosemary stepping down into the room. And whatever he had planned to say to her evaporated from his brain, because he'd never seen a sight more beautiful in his life. She was dressed in the color of sunshine, and surrounded by a delicate scent that reminded him for some reason of a field full of white wildflowers. And he asked himself yet again why he had pushed her away the other night, when she had been the one who had turned to him in a fit of need and desire.

Why?

He was no closer to an answer today than he had been

thirty-seven hours, fifty-eight minutes and six seconds ago. More than likely, it was because deep down inside himself, he knew there was no way on earth that Rosemary March could ever genuinely want him. But if that was true, then why had she come onto him the other night, if not because she was falling for him?

Why?

Unfortunately, he was confident he did know the answer to that question. Because of some damned comet, that's why.

Willis told himself it was stupid—not to mention in no way scientific—to think that Bobrzynyckolonycki might have had something to do with Rosemary's reactions to him the other night. Despite all the folklore, comets simply were not responsible for all the things people accused them of causing. But he had gone around and around in his head where his romantic experience with Rosemary was concerned, over and over again. And nothing about it made sense.

What had happened had been completely unanticipated and completely unprecedented. There had been no buildup, no warning, no time for him to prepare. It had just... happened. For no reason he could fathom. And somehow, he was absolutely certain it would never happen again. Not in a million years.

Or, at least, not in another fifteen.

Rosemary's response to him the other night had been in no way normal. Therefore, he'd been forced to conclude, it must have been influenced by something *ab*normal. Something completely out of the ordinary. Something *extra*ordinary. Or, maybe, something extraterrestrial.

At the very least, Rosemary had succumbed to the power of suggestion. In spite of his scientific convictions to the contrary, Willis had long ago noticed and accepted the fact that the good citizens of Endicott did indeed behave strangely whenever Bobrzynyckolonycki made an appearance. He'd noted it upon the comet's last approach to the planet, when he was thirteen years old, and he'd noted it again this year. People did in fact act funny during years of the comet. Period.

However, Willis was more of the opinion that they did so

not because of any cosmic influence the comet might have over them, but rather because people's subconscious minds allowed them to be swayed toward odd behavior. Because people had heard over and over again that the comet would make them do strange things, they did. They spoke their minds, wrecked their cars, had affairs, broke minor laws. And then they blamed it on Bobrzynyckolonycki.

And Rosemary, thanks to her below-average mental functioning, was doubtless more likely to succumb to such behavior than other people were. Since she'd been told continuously that she would be susceptible to strange behavior, perhaps even an odd love match, during the comet's appearance, she was letting herself think she was attracted to Willis. But once Bobrzynyckolonycki passed the earth and went hurtling on toward the sun, her subconscious would tell her the coast was clear, and that it was okay for her to go back to her usual pastimes.

In short, once Bobrzynyckolonycki was gone, Rosemary would hate Willis's guts again. It was that simple. Willis was convinced of it.

But looking at her now, seeing how beautiful, how warm, how sensuous she looked, he wanted to kick himself again for pushing her away. If there was even the smallest chance that she might eventually fall for him the way he had fallen for her all those years ago…

He sighed heavily and shoved the thought aside. Comet-inspired affection or not, Rosemary wasn't the woman for him. Because beauty, warmth and sensuality, although very nice to find in a potential mate, weren't nearly enough to keep a healthy relationship going for the long term. Whatever physical response he had to Rosemary—and granted, it was a pretty substantial physical response—in the long term, it just wouldn't be enough. Ultimately, beauty dimmed, warmth cooled and sensuality faded. There had to be more than that to keep two people together.

She took a few steps toward him, but halted when half the room's width still lay between them. "You said you wanted to talk about...us?'' she asked, stumbling a bit over the last word.

But Willis had stopped wanting to talk about the other night the minute she stepped into a pool of sunlight and became a part of it. Whatever dumb excuse he had been about to utter for his withdrawal from her the other night, whatever lame apology he had been about to voice for saying the unforgivable things he'd said afterward... All of it dried up in his throat.

Instead, all he could say was, ''Where are you going?''

She eyed him coolly for a moment, then told him, ''Angie's wedding.''

He eyed her back, quizzically. ''Angie? Your friend Angie? Angie Ellison?''

She nodded stiffly once.

''I didn't know she was getting married.''

Rosemary smiled tightly. ''Neither did I. Neither did Kirby. Neither did anybody in Endicott. Not until two days ago.''

Willis narrowed his eyes at her. ''Surely there must have been some indication. How long have she and her fiancé known each other?''

She seemed to be tallying mentally, so Willis said nothing to interrupt. After a few moments, she told him, ''I think they met formally about a week ago. When Angie broke into his house.''

Willis's eyebrows shot up at that. ''Excuse me? Angie did what?''

But instead of clarifying, Rosemary went on, ''It's crazy. She just called out of the blue on Thursday and told us all she was getting married Saturday at 2 p.m. at the Methodist Church—and she's not even Methodist, Willis, which makes no sense at all—oh, and by the way, she's registered at Michaelson's for Wedgwood and Waterford, but hey, don't worry about the price, because they have a club plan—twelve months, equal installments, no interest.''

Willis said nothing as he tried to process this wealth of information as quickly as possible. Then he realized Rosemary had neglected to mention one minor detail about the event. ''Who's she marrying?''

Rosemary shook her head and rolled her eyes heavenward. "The mob. Angie's marrying the mob."

Well, that certainly put anything he might have had to say about his own relationship with Rosemary in a very pale light. "*What?*"

Rosemary nodded. "She's marrying a lowlife, scumbag, murdering slug named Ethan Zorn, who also happens to be a mobster out to steal her father's pharmaceutical company, which he and his slug companions intend to use as a front for their filthy drug trade, can you believe it?"

Willis shook his head. "Rosemary, that makes no sense."

She gaped at him. "I know that. Don't you think I know that?"

"Well...does Angie know he's a mobster?"

"Yes!" Rosemary cried. "That's what's so crazy about this thing!"

Willis thought there was actually quite a bit more about this thing than that one item that was crazy, but he didn't say that to Rosemary.

She sighed helplessly and ran a restive hand through her hair. "Okay, I admit the guy she's marrying is sort of gorgeous in a dark, brooding, I'm-gonna-make-you-an-offer-you-can't-refuse kind of way, but honestly, Willis. He's a criminal! And she's marrying him! Today!"

All the fight seemed to go out of her—or at least, whatever fight she'd had left for Willis—and she strode to the couch and collapsed onto it. She stretched her legs—those long, slim, curvy, golden-tanned, luscious legs that had been straddling his mere hours ago—out in front of herself and sighed again.

Willis swallowed hard and forced his thoughts back to the matter at hand. "Why?" he asked. "Why would she marry such a man?"

Rosemary waved a hand airily toward the room at large. "Oh, just because some slant noses from South Philly will riddle her with enough bullets to qualify her for Swiss-cheese status if she doesn't marry him. Is that a crummy reason to get married or what? I mean, it's not like she's pregnant, for God's sake."

"Maybe I should go with you."

She snapped her attention back to Willis. "Go with me?" she repeated.

He nodded. "I don't like the idea of you being unescorted around a bunch of slant noses from South Philly."

Her eyebrows arrowed downward at that, making her look as if he'd hurt her feelings somehow with his offer. "What do you care if I take up with a bunch of slant noses?"

He supposed she had every right to ask that, considering how he'd behaved the other night. But all he said was, "I just don't think it's a good idea for you to go to this thing alone. Not with people like that there."

"What if I don't want to go with you?"

"Then I'll just invite myself and crash the thing and glue myself to your side. But don't worry," he added before she could come up with an excuse to put him off, "I'll stop by Michaelson's on the way and pick up a gravy boat or something."

She watched him warily for a minute, then glanced at the clock on the mantel. When she met his gaze again, her expression was inscrutable, and he wished he could look into her mind—however muddled and incoherent a place it probably was—and see what she was thinking.

"Well, you better hurry up," she finally told him. "We'll have to leave in about fifteen minutes if we're going to hit Michaelson's on the way."

"I'll be ready in ten," he assured her over his shoulder as he headed for the stairs.

With a gaily wrapped gravy boat tucked under one arm, and Rosemary clinging to the other, Willis entered the cavernous, festively decorated reception hall with some trepidation. And not because half the people present seemed to be wearing pointy-toed Italian shoes and reeking of pesto, either. But because he and Rosemary had made it through almost two full hours without sniping at each other once, and he had the feeling that such a truce wasn't going to last much longer.

Forget the mob, he thought as he made a quick inventory

of breast pockets in search of suspicious-looking bulges. It was Rosemary March, completely unarmed, whom Willis Random was afraid of.

"So," he began, "should we give our best wishes to the bride and groom?"

Rosemary shook her head. "No way. I don't want to get any closer to that guy than I have to. I don't care what Angie says. He doesn't look harmless to me. I'll talk to her when I can catch her alone."

Willis nodded, but he was rather of the opinion that the big, dark-haired man at Angie's side didn't look all *that* menacing. Still, it was probably better not to get any closer than was necessary to organized crime. You never could tell with mobsters.

"Then how about if we find a place to sit that's as far removed from the festivities as possible?" he suggested.

"Sounds good to me."

He deposited the gift on a table covered with pink crepe paper that had evidently been designated as such a repository, recalling with an odd thrill that he and Rosemary had chipped in together for it and both had signed the card. The gesture made them a couple somehow, and Willis was strangely delighted by that realization. Inevitably, he recalled again his withdrawal from her two nights ago, and again, he asked himself if he had lost his brilliant mind.

On the contrary, he assured himself. Keeping Rosemary beyond an arm's length was the only thing that would preserve his brilliant mind. As long as he was preoccupied by thoughts of getting up close and personal with her, he wouldn't be able to perform the job he'd come to Endicott to perform. He was here to study Bobrzynyckolonycki, not play touchy-feely with Rosemary March.

Even if touching her and feeling her had been pleasant beyond belief.

He squeezed his eyes shut tight and told himself that what he needed to do was focus his mind utterly and irrevocably on the more intellectual matters at hand. Tonight was the night that Bobrzynyckolonycki would be making its closest pass to the planet. He wouldn't have another chance like this one for fifteen years. And he couldn't afford to blow it by spending his time fantasizing about Rosemary March.

Unfortunately, the band on the other side of the reception hall chose that moment to strike up a slow, sensuous number, and he found himself wanting to dance. Which was truly bizarre, because Willis *never* danced. He was a terrible dancer, unable to master even the simplest step, and there was absolutely no way on earth that he would ever humiliate himself in public by asking a woman to dance with him. Especially a woman like Rosemary, who doubtless flowed as elegantly and fluidly across a dance floor as expensive champagne.

So it came as a very big surprise to him indeed when he leaned toward her and asked softly, "Would you like to dance?"

He shut his eyes tight again and gritted his teeth hard. How could he possibly have asked her such a question? he demanded of himself. Immediately, he began to send her silent thought waves that instructed her to answer him in the negative, even though, as a man of science, he knew things like ESP were complete hooey.

Don't dance with me, Rosemary, he mused emphatically. *Don't dance with me. Don't dance.... No, Willis, I don't want to dance. No, Willis, not with you. Forget it, Willis. I won't dance. I won't. I won't. No. No. No....*

She gazed at him blankly for a moment, then shook her head slowly. "Um, no. I don't think so."

Willis arched his eyebrows in surprise. Wow. It worked. Maybe Rosemary's brain wasn't as inactive as he thought. However, instead of feeling relieved by her decline of his offer, he felt somehow very disappointed. He was about to do something unbelievably stupid—like ask her again—when a newcomer approached their table.

"Yo, babe," the man said jovially.

Willis glanced up to find a very large, gorilla-like creature dressed in a dark, double-breasted suit of assumed Italian origin smiling lustily down at Rosemary. And even though the big man clearly wasn't addressing Willis—Willis may have been a lot of things, but "babe" wasn't one of them—he was the one to reply to the summons.

"Is there something you wanted?" he asked, forcing himself to be polite.

"Yeah," the man said genially. "I wanna dance wid your date." He stuck his hand out pleasantly and smiled. "Name's Eddie. But most people call me 'Slant Nose.'"

Willis's eyebrows shot up at that, and he saw immediately why the nickname had come about. "Uh...nice to meet you, um...Slant Nose, but, uh..." He glanced over at Rosemary to find her gaping at their new companion, her eyes wide with terror. "Um," he continued, "my, uh, date here and I were just going to dance ourselves. Isn't that right, Rosemary?"

This time when he looked over at her, it was to find her nodding vigorously, her dark curls bouncing wildly with the action. "Uh-huh," she said with false brightness. She looped her arm around Willis's and yanked him close. "Willis and I are going to be dancing every single dance together, aren't we, honey?" She smiled again, a dazzling smile that he could almost convince himself was genuine. Then she tilted her head to rest it on his shoulder. After a wistful little sigh, she added, "We're in love."

Slant Nose smiled back. "Aw, dat's so cute. I love it when two people fall in love. Some udder time den. Mebbe I can dance wid da bride at your wedding, huh?"

Willis and Rosemary nodded quickly in unison.

"Congrats," Slant Nose added with a wave as he departed. "You make a lovely couple."

They remained silent until he was out of sight, then Willis muttered, "I think that was the singularly most bizarre encounter I've ever experienced."

Rosemary's fingers convulsed on his arm. "Dance with me. Now. Before any of those other guys come over." She stood and scooted her chair away from the table with enough force to send it toppling over.

Willis looked up at her and had to bite back his own wistful little sigh that threatened to erupt. God, even standing in fear of the mob, she was so beautiful. *We're in love,* she had told

Slant Nose. A funny little flutter danced in his belly when he remembered the words, and he found himself wishing they were true. But Rosemary March would never fall in love with someone like him. Not under normal circumstances, anyway.

He expelled a soft breath of air and forced a smile in response to her own. Then he stood and followed her toward the parquetry laid down at the center of the room to accommodate the dancers. When she turned around, he settled one hand gently on her hip and pressed the other against her open palm. A good six inches separated their bodies as they began to sway, and Willis tried to forget that he had absolutely no idea what he was doing.

"Willis?"

She spoke his name so low he almost missed hearing it. But the sound of her voice pulled him out of his troubling reverie, and he focused his gaze on her face. Her brown eyes were brimming with an emotion he didn't even want to contemplate, and her lips were parted slightly, as if she were about to say something, but wasn't certain the observation would be welcome.

"What?" he asked softly.

"You seem so far away," she said. "What are you thinking about?"

He wondered what she would say if he told her he'd been thinking about how much he wanted her, about how much he wished she would like him, about how difficult it was for him to be back in Endicott as a grown man who was still completely infatuated with her. How would she react if he told her he'd been thinking about the fact that he'd wanted to make love to her the other night, as badly as she'd seemed to want him?

Unfortunately, the operative word here was *seemed*. Rosemary honestly *seemed* interested in him. She *seemed* to truly like him. She *seemed* as willing to get more seriously involved as he was. But that was it. She *seemed* all those things. She wasn't actually experiencing them. Not genuinely. She felt that way only because her subconscious mind told her to surrender to an imagined cosmic influence that drew her to a man she would normally never find attractive.

Yes, Rosemary *seemed* to want him. But she didn't. Not really. Not the way he wanted her.

He forced a cheerfulness that he didn't feel into his voice when he told her, "I was just thinking that tonight's the night."

She eyed him warily at that. "What do you mean?"

He eyed her back, wondering what that speculative, hopeful little gleam in her eye was all about. He shrugged. "I mean...tonight's the night," he repeated.

"What night?"

"*The* night."

"Willis, what are you talking about?"

"Bobrzynyckolonycki," he told her. "Tonight's the night that the comet makes its closest pass to the earth. What did you think I was talking about?"

She inhaled a deep breath and released it quickly, her dark eyes now reflecting her obvious disappointment in his answer. "Well, there are those who might recall a certain song from our school days and think something else."

He smiled briefly, but felt confused. "What song?"

"That Rod Stewart song. 'Tonight's the Night.'"

"I don't remember that song."

"I'm not surprised. You never listened to anything as common as popular music on the radio."

"What was the song about?"

She shook her head. "Never mind."

Somehow, while they were chatting, their bodies had moved closer together, and now Willis realized the hand that he had placed gingerly on her hip was open palmed at the small of her back. Scarcely two inches separated them, and he could feel the heat of her body near his, could inhale the rich, sweet aroma of her perfume, could detect the whisper of her soft breath against his neck. And involuntarily, he pulled her even closer.

When he drew her body flush against him, Rosemary lifted her gaze to meet his, but she said nothing to even hint at what she might be thinking. So Willis pressed her closer still. Oddly, he didn't stumble once. Dancing with Rosemary felt like the most natural act in the world. He closed his fingers snugly over hers, drew his hand up between her shoulder blades and spun her around as if he were competing for the championship ballroom dancing title. Rosemary sank into him as if she were a part of him, following his lead beautifully, as if the two of them danced this way all the time.

Too soon, the song ended, and a hazy silence settled over the room. But instead of springing apart, they stood perfectly still, arms entwined, each caught in the other's gaze. And as he had two nights ago, Willis felt himself falling into the dark depths of Rosemary's eyes as if helpless to stop himself. Just as he had that night, he suddenly forgot all about their differences. He forgot that her brain wasn't nearly stimulating enough for his, forgot that he was supposed to keep her at arm's length, forgot that she would go back to hating his guts the minute Bobrzynyckolonycki left the earth's orbit.

And he remembered how it had felt to hold her half-naked in his arms while she plundered his mouth with hers.

Then he felt himself leaning toward her, holding her hand more tightly, roping his arm more resolutely around her waist, pulling her closer...closer...closer...

"*There* you guys are! I've been looking all over for you. No wonder I couldn't find you. The dance floor is the *last* place I would have looked."

Still feeling a little dazed, Willis turned to find Rosemary's friend Kirby swooping down on them like a guardian angel. She looked truly ethereal, wearing a flowered dress he could only call dainty, her white blond hair swept back from her delicate oval face with a black velvet headband. So angelic did she look, in fact, that she could have passed as the poster child for Virginity International. Which of course would be appropriate, because everyone in Endicott knew that Kirby Connaught had never done *that,* not once in her entire life. Not that she hadn't tried.

"Kirb!" Rosemary called out to her friend.

Quickly and completely, she disengaged herself from Willis's embrace, looking as if she'd just been caught committing the most heinous crime. "I, uh…"

She colored and glanced away from Willis's face, and something twisted painfully inside him.

"I've been looking all over for you, too," she told Kirby.

Kirby eyed the two of them suspiciously. "You didn't look like you were looking for me. You look like you only have eyes for Wil—"

"Can you believe Angie actually went through with it?" Rosemary cut her friend off. "She's actually married to the mob now!"

Kirby crossed her arms over her chest and sighed hard. "I know. I can't believe no one stood up when the minister said all that 'Speak now' stuff."

As one, the two women turned and gazed angrily at Willis. For a moment, he didn't know what they were mad about. Then he understood. *"Me?"* he exclaimed. "Why should *I* have stood up and objected? It's none of *my* business who Angie decides to marry."

Both women gaped at him.

"Willis," Rosemary said. "We're talking about the mob here. The *mob.*"

"I know," he told her emphatically. "That's what I mean. Why should I have been the one to stand in the line of fire? You two are her friends."

"Oh, you are just *so* gallant."

He shook his head. "Angie's a big girl," he stated. "If she didn't want to marry the guy, she didn't have to. You ask me, the way she and her new husband have been looking at each other, *they* would have been the ones to draw a weapon if anyone had objected to the union."

Rosemary shook her head at Willis but didn't contradict him. "Angie does seem awfully captivated by that lowlife, scumbag, murdering slug Ethan Zorn," she muttered. "I think the real problem is that she just hasn't been getting any lately." Then she turned to her other friend. "No offense, Kirb."

Kirby nodded and sighed wistfully, her expression one of resignation. ''None taken.''

''We need to go talk to her,'' Rosemary said.

Kirby nodded, and without a word to Willis, the two women linked their arms and strode off toward the bride and groom. And all he could do was watch them leave, thinking that Angie Ellison Zorn wasn't the only person in Endicott who hadn't been getting any lately. And maybe that absence of... uh...activity—and *not* a comet's influence—was what was really causing Willis and Rosemary to respond to each other the way they had been.

In which case, he thought further, maybe they were both long overdue....

Eight

Eight

The sun was hanging low in the sky by the time Rosemary and Willis arrived home. Angie and her mobster husband had left the reception hours before, and Rosemary refused to even contemplate what the night ahead held for her friend.

Never mind that Angie had assured her and Kirby that there was nothing to fear. Never mind that toward the end of the reception, Angie had intimated to her two best friends that she was actually kind of looking forward to getting to know her new husband better. Never mind that, while the three women were in the ladies' room, Angie had lifted her skirt to reveal a skimpy little white garter belt and white fishnet stockings that she'd purchased just that afternoon in anticipation of her wedding night.

Never mind that one of Rosemary's best friends in the world was convinced that she was falling in love with a criminal, when all that was really happening was that Angie was under the influence of some stupid chunk of glowing ice and debris surfing through the cosmos.

Rosemary couldn't think about all that right now. Because she was too busy trying not to fall in love herself.

To stave off her worries about Angie—not to mention herself—she had consumed more than her fair share of champagne. She told herself the wine was the only thing that had kept her nerves steady while guys who had introduced themselves with names like Manny the Meat Hook and Two-Fingers Nick had kept asking her to dance. Willis had played the part of her paladin all night long, and had laid his life on the line to keep them all at bay.

He had danced with her every single dance.

And the more she had danced with Willis, the more Rosemary had come to realize that, as stupid as it was to do, she was, without question, falling in love with him. And worse than that, unlike Angie's, her emotions had absolutely nothing to do with a comet.

"Willis?" she said as she closed and locked the front door behind them.

He spun around at the summons, looking tired and rumpled and very endearing. In his outfit of brown trousers and brown tweed jacket, accessorized by a brown necktie and his ever-present glasses, he looked every inch the stuffy college professor. But Rosemary knew he wasn't stuffy. Beneath that frumpy, intellectual exterior raged the heart of a man whose appetites were fierce. If only he would let her feed that hunger.

"Yes?" he asked, clearly distracted.

She eyed him thoughtfully, not sure exactly how to conclude what had been a surprisingly nice day with him. Part of her thought it probably wouldn't be a good idea to spend any more time with Willis than she already had, because they were bound to start sniping at each other again soon if their contact was further prolonged. But part of her—a pretty big part of her, in fact—wanted the day to go on forever.

"I, uh…" she began clumsily. Then she decided to just plunge in. "It's not quite dark yet. There's some wine in the fridge, if you'd like another glass."

He lifted his hand, palm out. "No, thank you. I think I had

more than my fair share at the reception. One more glass, and we would have had to take a taxi home.''

She nodded, then lifted a hand to rub anxiously at her forehead. "I just can't stop thinking about Angie with that... that...that lowlife, scumbag, murdering slug.''

Willis smiled. "Look, if it's any consolation, I actually did spend some time talking to the guy. Frankly, Rosemary, I'm not convinced he's such a bad sort.''

She gaped at him. "Willis! He's a criminal.''

"He told me he's a sales rep for the Cokely Chemical Corporation.''

Rosemary waved a hand in dismissal. "Oh, that's just his cover.''

Willis smiled a reassuring smile. "Angie certainly seems to like him.''

Rosemary shook her head. "No, Angie seems to actually love him.''

"Then what's the problem?''

She studied him in silence for a moment, suddenly feeling at one with her friend. Because just like Angie, Rosemary had fallen in love with a man who was completely inappropriate for her. And even if Willis wasn't a mobster, he was every bit as dangerous in his own way. Because he could hurt her deeply if she let him.

"The problem is that he's dangerous, and he could hurt her," she said softly, speaking her thoughts aloud.

Willis shook his head. "He's not going to hurt her. And he doesn't seem at all the dangerous type to me. He looks perfectly innocent.''

Rosemary smiled weakly. "The innocent-looking ones are the ones you have to watch out for.''

He eyed her in puzzlement, then glanced over his shoulder toward the stairs. "I need to get up to the attic," he told her. "It's not dark yet, but it will be before long. I need to get things ready.''

"Can I come with you?''

The question was out of her mouth before she could stop it, but once uttered, she realized she had no desire to take it back. Angie's wedding, for all the weirdness of it, had still been festive and fun, and Rosemary didn't quite want to let go of that celebratory feeling. She didn't want to be all by herself downstairs with no companion but two cats and a low-budget horror movie. She was tired of spending her nights alone.

Willis, too, seemed surprised by her question, but he lifted a shoulder idly and let it drop. "Sure. Why not?"

"I won't be in your way?" she asked.

He shook his head. "No, Rosemary. You won't be in my way." Then he lifted a hand to his necktie. "I just need to change my clothes," he said, struggling to free the knot. Unfortunately, the knot wouldn't loosen, and he began to fight more desperately with it.

"Here, let me help you," Rosemary told him when she noted his struggles, drawing nearer.

He seemed wary of her offer at first, but relinquished the necktie to her care. She tucked a finger underneath and began to gently loosen the knot, tugging harder when the bond refused to budge. She took another step forward and brought her other hand into the effort, working more diligently at the tightly wound tie. As she fumbled, she gradually began to realize how close she was standing to Willis. His outdoorsy, masculine scent surrounded her, and the heat of his big body enveloped her. His breathing seemed to be coming in irregular little gasps all of a sudden, his throat working convulsively against the collar of his shirt.

She chuckled a little anxiously. "Jeez, Willis, who taught you how to tie a tie? And since when did you stop wearing clip-ons?"

He, too, laughed, but the sound was forced, strained. "I was in a hurry this afternoon. I guess I wasn't paying attention to how I was tying it. Ow!" His hands immediately joined hers, covering her fumbling fingers. "Rosemary! You're cutting off my breath!"

"Maybe I should get some scissors," she said as she loosened the tie some. He inhaled a deep, quick breath and relaxed a little. But still the knot refused to come completely free.

"Absolutely not," he told her. "You're not coming anywhere near this tie with a pair of scissors. This is my best tie."

She paused in her actions and gaped at him. "This is your best tie? *This?* Willis, this is the ugliest tie I've ever seen. It's polyester, for God's sake."

He looked down at her, clearly insulted. "Excuse me, but I bought this tie at one of the finest discount stores in Boston. It cost me almost fifteen dollars."

She rolled her eyes and shook her head. "You need someone to look after you. Preferably someone with good taste."

She halted her actions immediately when she realized what she had just implied. Hoping he hadn't been paying attention, she forced her gaze up to his, her fingers still twisted in the length of his tie. Unfortunately, Willis was gazing back down at her very intently. And although he said nothing to acknowledge that he had heard what she said, she could see by the glitter of fire in his eyes that her words had most definitely registered.

"I mean…" she began, working at the knot in his tie once more. "That is, I…uh… I'm not suggesting that *I* be the one to look after you. Just that *someone* ought to—"

"Oh, I don't know, Rosemary," he interrupted her. "I think you have good taste." He paused a telling moment before adding, "I thought you tasted pretty good the other night."

Her hands faltered in their progress when he said it, and a burst of fire licked at her belly. But she forced herself not to succumb. Instead, she pretended she hadn't heard him, and focused on freeing the knot at his throat. Finally, finally, she managed to unloop the tightest part, and then the rest of the knot fell free. But she didn't stop tugging until both ends of the tie hung unfettered from his collar.

"There," she said, hoping she only imagined the breathlessness she heard in her voice.

Instead of turning loose of his tie, however, her fingers curled more tightly over it. Willis's hands covered hers, and when she looked up at his face, she saw that he was smiling at her. A genuine, *Hey-you're-all-right-you-know-that?* kind of smile that curled her toes and took her breath away.

"Did you hear what I said?" he asked her softly.

She didn't answer him. She couldn't. All she could do was stare at him in silence, and try not feel the way she was starting to feel.

"You really do taste good," he repeated. "Good enough to…"

His voice trailed off, and suddenly Rosemary was moving closer to him. But she wasn't the one doing the pulling this time. Willis was. The hands covering hers curved more tightly over her fingers, and he slid her hands down along the length of his tie. When she no longer had the comfort of the fabric to clutch in her hands, Rosemary automatically curled her fingers into loose fists. Until Willis effortlessly uncurled them and lifted them to the back of his neck. Then he bent his head forward and covered her mouth with his.

This time Willis was the one to initiate the kiss. Rosemary was sure of it. He flattened her palms over his nape, and when she pressed her fingers into his warm flesh, he skimmed his hands back down along her bare arms. Then he looped his own arms around her waist, pulled her close and kissed her again.

Immediately, Rosemary melted into him, wanting to seize the moment for as long as she could. His mouth on hers was warm and gentle, the tenderness in his embrace nearly undoing her. She had wanted him for what seemed like half a lifetime. And now he was coming to her, willingly, eagerly, lovingly. Willis had started it this time, she told herself again as delight rippled through her. And she couldn't help but wonder if he would finish it this time, too.

The memory of him pushing her away two nights before erupted in her brain then, and instinctively, she pulled her mouth from his. He followed her withdrawal, urging her body closer to his as he dipped his head toward hers again. But Rosemary doubled her fists loosely against his chest and ducked her head to the side before his lips could claim hers again.

"Don't do this to me, Willis," she pleaded softly. "Don't

kiss me this way and make me think you want me, then push me aside like you did the other night."

He halted his forward motion, then pulled back enough to meet her gaze levelly. "The other night..." he began, his voice drifting off before he completed whatever he had been about to say. He shook his head silently, almost imperceptibly.

She kept her forearms braced against his chest as a barrier—however futile—between them. "What about the other night?" she asked.

"I wasn't thinking straight," he told her.

She hesitated for a moment, then confessed, "Neither was I."

This time he nodded, and a shutter dropped over his eyes, obscuring whatever he might be feeling. He dropped his hands back to his sides and took a step backward. Immediately, she felt cold and alone.

"Then you don't want this," he said quietly.

She stepped forward again, unconsciously seeking his heat and closeness. "I didn't say that." She nibbled her lower lip thoughtfully, but didn't elaborate.

As if he didn't even realize he was doing it, he lifted his hand to her hair and wound a loose curl around his index finger. "Then what do you want, Rosemary?"

Worried that she was setting herself up for a fall, she deliberately turned the tables on him. "What do *you* want?"

He smiled halfheartedly and idly let drop the curl he had twisted around his finger. "I asked you first."

She tried to smile back, but wasn't sure she quite managed it. "I, um..." She shifted her weight from one foot to the other, then crossed her arms over her abdomen in a gesture of self-preservation. "I want, uh..." Restlessly, she shifted her weight again, then dropped her gaze to the floor. "I want you to kiss me again," she finally said softly. Then she glanced back up and met his gaze levelly. "And I want you to keep kissing me."

Immediately, he moved to stand in front of her, curling his index finger beneath her chin, gently tilting her head back until he could gaze down on her face. With his other hand, he reached up and removed his glasses, deftly folded them, then tucked them into his jacket pocket. She opened her palms over the soft fabric of his shirt, and instinctively, her fingers curled into the warm flesh she detected beneath. But as he bent his head to hers again, she pulled back one more time.

"But not if you're going to push me away," she told him. "Willis, please don't do that to me again."

He smiled at her, and pressed his forehead to hers. "I won't," he promised. "Rosemary, the other night..." He sighed heavily. "What I did was a stupid, thoughtless thing to do."

She still wasn't sure she trusted him. "Why do you say that? I've never heard you refer to yourself as stupid or thoughtless. On the contrary, everything you've ever said or done has been—"

"What else would you call it," he interrupted her, "when a man rejects a beautiful woman he's wanted for a long, long time?"

Something deep inside her twisted fiercely, and she was about to ask him just exactly how long he'd been wanting her. Days? Weeks? Years? What? But before she could utter the question, he dipped his head to hers again and covered her mouth with his.

"I want you, Rosemary," he said softly against her lips after kissing her briefly, gently, tentatively. "And I can tell you want me. Why should we deny each other? Why not just enjoy this while we can, even if we don't for a moment understand it?"

She chuckled softly, a little nervously. "That doesn't sound like the brilliant scientist talking. That sounds more like something *I* would say. Where's all the calculation and the formulation and the math? How can you let yourself get caught up in something like this, something that makes no sense? Something that defies explanation?"

He smiled. "Blame it on Bobrzynyckolonycki."

Although he clearly meant his comment in jest, something about it bothered Rosemary. But before she had a chance to consider it, Willis kissed her again, a deep, drugging, demanding kiss, and she ceased to think at all. Instead, she looped her arms around his neck and pulled him closer, and lost herself in his kiss.

Willis, too, felt lost, and had for some time now. He tried to pinpoint when exactly he'd surrendered control of the situation, certain it must have been very recently, sometime while he and Rosemary had been dancing at Angie's wedding reception. But as she kissed him back with a genuine need and desire and affection that he couldn't possibly ignore, he decided he'd never been even remotely in control where his feelings for her were concerned.

Suddenly, he felt like a thirteen-year-old boy again, holding a girl in his arms for the very first time. Except that where most adolescent boys had to be content with adolescent girls and the most rudimentary—and potentially malfunctioning—social and sexual skills, Willis had landed himself a full-blown woman with a fully working libido. And suddenly, he remembered something that might just ruin the evening.

Reluctantly, he pulled back from her again and said, "Uh, Rosemary?"

Her head was tipped back, her eyes were still closed and her lips were still puckered as she replied absently, "Hmmmm?"

"If what I think is going to happen is going to happen…"

Without opening her eyes, and in a dreamy little voice that ignited a raging fire in his belly, she said, "Oh, I think it's safe to assume that it's going to happen."

He cleared his throat a little awkwardly and told her, "Then there's something you should probably know about me."

Her eyes snapped open at that, and she pinned him with her gaze. "What?"

He swallowed hard. "I, uh…"

"What, Willis?"

"I've, um…" He inhaled deeply again and told himself to just spit it out. "I've only, uh…I've only been with two women before."

He thought she smiled at that, but he wasn't sure. So he quickly plunged ahead. "One was the accounting major I mentioned earlier, and the other was a calculus professor from MIT who ended up taking a position at Stanford a couple of years ago.''

This time he was sure Rosemary smiled. ''That's it?'' she asked. ''That's what I should know about you?''

He nodded. ''Yes. That's it. I've only had two lovers in my entire life, and if truth be told, neither of those relationships was in any way, uh...what you might call, um... That is, I never really felt particularly, well...with either one of them. I'm sorry I'm not more—''

She covered his mouth with two fingers, cutting him off in midblather, something for which he was profoundly grateful. Then she pushed herself up on tiptoe, removed her fingers and kissed him lightly on the lips. ''Don't apologize,'' she said. ''I'm glad.''

That surprised him. Surely a woman like Rosemary would want a man who knew what he was doing. ''You are?''

She nodded. ''I've only been with two men before.''

Now *that* really surprised him. ''You have?''

She looked dashed by the comment. ''Well, you don't have to sound like that.''

''Like what?''

''Like you assumed I'd been with dozens of men.''

He felt heat creep into his face, but he said nothing. Nevertheless, his guilt must have been evident, because Rosemary gaped at him, obviously reading his thoughts.

''Willis! How could you think that of me?''

''Well, look at you, Rosemary,'' he said in his defense. ''What man wouldn't want you?''

She, too, blushed, and some of her tension seemed to ease. ''For one thing, not that many. And for another, it takes a lot more than a man wanting me for me to...you know.''

''It does?''

''Of course it does. Just how shallow do you think I am?''

''I never meant to imply that you were shallow. Just that you were beautiful and desirable and warm and funny and wonderful and...'' He smiled. ''And that any man who came within a hundred miles of you would want you.''

Now she was definitely blushing, and the knowledge that he had been the one to cause her reaction made Willis feel like the greatest lover the world had ever known.

"Well, most men aren't interested," she told him softly. "And I haven't been interested in most men."

He wanted to ask her why, then decided he'd better not push his luck. What was important right now was that Rosemary wanted him. He didn't care why or how long it would last. He didn't question whatever twist of fate or the cosmos had brought the two of them together like this. He only knew that to ignore this opportunity to be with her would make him the most insipid idiot on the planet. Willis was a smart guy. And he wasn't about to walk away from what Rosemary was offering.

So he pulled her close again, kissed her deeply and forgot about everything else in the universe.

Her hands at his nape tightened, pulling him closer, then one wandered to the button at his throat and deftly unfastened it. Another followed, then another and another, and with each one she freed, Willis deepened their kiss. She opened her mouth to him willingly, urging him inside, tangling her tongue with his as they warred for possession of the embrace.

When she loosed the final button on his shirt and jerked his shirttail free of his trousers, she shoved it and his jacket off his shoulders, letting them fall to the floor. He leaned forward, bending her back over the arm he had looped around her waist. Then he lifted his hand to the big button at her neckline and, with one flick of his fingers, slipped it through the buttonhole that held it. Before he lost his nerve, he moved quickly to the next and unfastened it, as well, then moved down to the third.

A whisper of her perfume assailed him as the fabric of her dress folded back over his hand, exposing her warm flesh. And his fingers trembled over the fourth button as he pondered exactly what to do next.

Then Rosemary covered his hand with hers, and she lifted his fingers away from the button, tucking them beneath the opening of her dress. She cupped them insistently over the pink lace of her brassiere, and Willis felt heat pool in his groin as he closed his palm over her warm flesh. For one long moment, he only held her that way, still stunned by the knowledge that he was standing here with her like this, with nothing obstructing what he had wanted for so long. Then he curved his fingers into her soft breast, pressed his palm insistently against the quickly ripening peak and took possession.

Rosemary emitted a soft sound that was part sigh, part groan, part demand for more. Willis tore his mouth from hers, and he buried his face against the heated skin of her neck. He dragged erratic, desperate kisses along the slender column of her throat, tasted the delicate hollow at its base and then moved lower, to the dusky valley between her breasts. Rosemary tangled her fingers in his hair and held him there, and he roped his arms around her waist to draw her closer still. He covered her breast with his mouth, suckling her through the lace, her nipple growing stiff and alive with his ministrations.

"Oh," she said above him. "Oh, Willis…"

He reached for the front closure of her brassiere and unhooked it, then pushed the film of lace aside. With her bared to him in such a way, he could only stare in wonder for a moment, at once humbled by the gift she was bestowing upon him and greedy to have more. For a brief moment, he only pressed his cheek to her naked breast, closed his eyes and reveled in the feel of her fingers stroking his hair. Then he ducked his head and drew her into his mouth again, holding her breast with sure fingers, laving her, sucking her, pulling her deep inside him.

"Oh, *Willis*…" she repeated more urgently, tightening her fingers in his hair.

He smiled in spite of himself, flicked his tongue over her warm flesh and freed button number four. The rest of her buttons quickly followed, until she stood before him with her dress gaping open over little more than a wispy triangle of lace that hugged her lower torso. As she had done to him only moments before, he shoved the garment over her shoulders and down to the floor. He felt her tugging at his belt, freeing the length of leather from its buckle, then her fingers at his waistband, struggling with the button of his trousers.

Just as she began to tug the zipper down, he circled her wrist with strong fingers and pulled her hand away. She glanced up at him, obviously worried that he was about to break his promise and call a halt to their activities. He smiled, knowing nothing could be further from the truth.

And quickly, he clarified, "Your room or mine?"

Nine

She smiled back at him. "What's wrong with the living-room floor?"

He arched his eyebrows in surprise at her boldness, then tilted his head toward the window seat. "We have company."

She glanced over and smiled at the two cats that were observing the action with expressions of utter boredom. "You're right," she said. "They'd probably only laugh at us. And then they'd cheapen it even more by talking about it with all their cat friends. It would be all over the neighborhood by tomorrow morning." She turned her attention back to Willis. "I'll let you choose. Your room or mine?"

He smiled as whimsy got the better of him, and he scooped her up into his arms. Her lips parted in surprise at the gesture, and he took advantage by covering her mouth with his and tasting her deeply. He didn't stop kissing her as he carried her up the stairs and into the guest room he had occupied for weeks. Nor did he stop kissing her as he laid her back on his bed. Instead, he fell right down onto the mattress beside her, urged her body closer to his own and kissed her again. And again. And again. And again.

Finally, Rosemary rolled to her back and pulled him atop her, roping one arm around his neck, splaying her other hand open over his naked back. His skin was hot and hard where she touched him, soft silk covering tempered steel. His hands seemed to be everywhere—in her hair, on her breasts, under her bottom—and every time he moved, she felt the ripple of muscles dancing beneath her fingertips. His mouth was on her throat, her shoulder, her breasts, her belly, then she felt him venturing lower. He snagged the edge of her panties in one fist and jerked them down, over her hips, along her legs, until they joined her shoes on the floor.

And then she felt his mouth on her legs, tasting her calves, her knees, her thighs, moving higher and higher, pausing at a place where no man had tarried before. When she understood his intention, something in her stomach knotted fiercely. "Willis…" she whispered with a gasp, the single word both a warning and a plea.

"Shh," he replied, covering her thighs with his big hands, urging her legs open wider.

"But, Willis…"

"Shh…"

He murmured the sound against her inner thigh, then against the damp, heated core of her. Before she could say another word, he dipped his head again, tasting her more intimately than she could ever have imagined. A wildfire shot through her at the touch, paralyzing her for a moment. Then the heat leveled off, meandered from her belly to her extremities, and all she could do was feel.

She was vaguely conscious of tangling her fingers in his hair, of bending her knees and lifting her hips, of glancing down to see his dark head making circular motions against her. Then she closed her eyes and surrendered to the play of light and color and sensation dancing in her brain. And just when she thought she could tolerate no more, Willis began to move back up her body, dragging his open mouth along the heated flesh of her torso, tasting her breasts again, then coming to rest at her mouth.

"Rosemary March, you are one sexy woman," he whispered against her jaw.

All she could manage in response was a murmur of delight and a dreamy little smile of contentment. But that contentment was short-lived, lasting only as long as it took Willis to shuck his trousers and briefs and come to rest between her legs again. She felt him ripe and stiff against her, and instinctively, she reached down to caress him. He groaned as she skimmed her fingertips along his hard length, and she gasped when she realized the extent of his arousal.

"Obviously, you didn't build that big telescope of yours because of any masculine, uh…shortcomings," she said with a smile and a salacious little chuckle.

The grin he threw her in response was self-satisfied, almost smug. "I've come a long way since high school," he told her.

She laughed again. "I'll say."

Completely without hesitation or inhibition, he covered her breast with sure fingers and squeezed gently. "But then, so have you. I distinctly remember you as a B cup."

She gaped at him, first shocked, then amused. "Why, Willis, I didn't know you'd noticed."

In response to her statement, he kissed her again, not a passionate, fiery, barely controlled kiss, as so many of the others had been, but a gentle, tender brush of his lips against hers. When he pulled back, he gazed steadily into her eyes and told her, "More than you know, Rosemary. More than you know."

Before she could ponder the import of his words, he moved atop her, nestling between her legs. Instinctively, she looped her calves over his, and stroked him again with sure fingers, rubbing her hand slowly along the length of him until he began to move his body in rhythm with her caresses. For long moments, they simply lay so entwined, then, without warning, Willis removed her hand and rolled to his back, bringing Rosemary with him for the ride. Then he settled his hands at her waist and slowly scooted her backward, until she was sitting astride him.

She curled her fingers in the dark, springy hair that covered his chest, then lifted her hips toward that hard, heavy part of him that beckoned to her. As one, they joined their bodies together, each murmuring in satisfaction as he filled her. Slowly, Willis penetrated her softness, sinking deeper and deeper as Rosemary lowered herself down on top of him. She closed her eyes and dug her fingers into his chest as slowly, oh so slowly, she buried the last of him inside her.

"Oh…" she whispered. "Oh, Willis…"

At his gentle urging, she rose up on her knees, the friction of his withdrawal making her whole body shudder. Then she plunged back down over him, taking him more deeply still. Little by little, they set a pace that grew steadily more rhythmic, more demanding, more fierce. A hot coil inside her began to wind tighter and tighter, threatening to explode in a crash of heat at any moment. And just when she thought that moment was coming, Willis shifted their bodies until she was beneath him.

He splayed his hands open on each side of her head and rose above her, but he never withdrew from her. "Rosemary," he whispered. "Open your eyes. Look at me."

She did as he instructed and met his gaze evenly, but she couldn't find the strength to utter a word. Instead she reached up and threaded her fingers through his hair, and hoped he could understand how very much she loved him.

"I want to watch you," he said, his breathing ragged, his voice rough. "And I want you to see me when we…oh… Oh, Rosemary…"

He cried out as his voice trailed off and his motions grew more frantic. He rose to his knees and moved his hands to her hips, lifting her from the bed so that he could enter her more deeply still. Dismayed that she couldn't reach him, Rosemary gripped the rails of the headboard behind her and held on for dear life as he pelted her again and again. But her gaze never left his, and his never left hers. Not until a burst of white-hot sensation shot through her, and she threw her head back against the pillow and squeezed her eyes shut tight.

With one final thrust, Willis stilled, emptying himself inside her with a heat and rapidity unlike anything he had ever experienced before. For long moments, he knelt before her, waiting for the onslaught of sensation and emotion to end. Then he collapsed beside her, pulled her close and forced himself not to say the things he so desperately wanted to tell her.

Later, he vowed silently. When he understood those things himself. Later he could utter the words that he'd kept locked up tight inside for half his life. Later he could put voice to all the bizarre, inexplicable, wonderful things that had tied him up in knots for too long. Later he could bare his soul for all the world to see.

Later he could tell Rosemary he loved her.

Willis awoke slowly, only halfway sensing the presence of a warm, soft, body beside him in his bed. Heat suffused his belly and wound out toward his extremities as he gradually recalled the previous night's exploits. And, without bothering to open his eyes, he grinned with much satisfaction.

His misgivings about his own inexperience with women hadn't proved to be much of a problem, especially in light of Rosemary's comparable inexperience with men. Something had definitely come over both of them last night, some instinctive, primitive need and desire that had brought them together like two experts on the subject of lovemaking. His smile broadened as the memories overcame him one by leisurely one, of the numerous times they'd awaken in each other's arms only to exhaust themselves to the point of slumber again.

How strange that Rosemary hadn't taken more lovers in her life, when there surely could have been no shortage of suitors, he thought further. How strange…and how wonderful.

She still lay sleeping soundly next to him, her body tucked spoon-fashion against his. One of his hands was cupped gently over a bare breast, and the other was dangling over a naked hip. What a magnificent way to wake up, he thought. And how very glorious it would be to wake up in such a way every morning. He inhaled deeply the mingling fragrances of wild-flower and woman, and wondered how on earth he could have gotten so lucky. He was still smiling as he opened his eyes and squinted against the sunlight streaming through the lace curtains that hung over the window.

Sunlight. Oh, God, no.

He bolted upright in bed, then hastily scrambled out, knocking Rosemary over the other side in his hurry. Sunlight meant daybreak. And daybreak meant that he had completely missed Bobrzynckolonycki last night. Still not trusting his own eyes, Willis thrust his legs into a pair of sweatpants that hung over the arm of a nearby chair, then raced to the window and tore back the curtains. And then he stared wide-eyed and silent out at the sunny morning.

"Willis?"

He hung his head at the sound of his name on Rosemary's lips, cursing under his breath. How on earth had this happened? he demanded of himself. How had he let himself be so utterly distracted by her? How could he have spent the entire night wrapped up in her arms, in her softness, in her love, and missed out on the single most important event of his adult life? How could he have completely forgotten Bobrzynckolonycki? How could he have missed his chance to go down in history? *How on earth had this happened?*

"Willis?"

He spun quickly around, turning his back on the evidence of the dawning day, wishing like hell this had all been a bad dream, knowing, instead, that he had ruined everything. How was he supposed to explain this to his colleagues? To the press? To MIT? To the entire scientific community at large? Just what was he supposed to tell them?

Well, you know, I really meant *to take a look at that comet Bob thing on the most important night of its passing, but I sort of got involved with making love to a beautiful woman, instead. Sorry. Thanks for all the funding and interest, anyway. Maybe next time.*

Oh, yeah. That ought to go over real well with the global scientific community.

"Willis?"

The third time she spoke his name, he could sense something akin to panic in her voice. "What?" he bit out angrily in response.

She was kneeling on the other side of the bed, where she'd fallen when he'd leaped out, and was twisting the sheet ferociously in both fists. Her dark curls rioted atop her head, having clearly been enjoyed by the hands of an eager lover. Her dark eyes were brimming with concern and anxiety, and her mouth—that incredible, generous, erotic mouth—was thinned into a tight line.

She had made love to him without inhibition last night, he remembered as a mixture of affection and frustration warred in his belly. And because of his fascination with her, he had failed to make the most important discovery of his career, the discovery he had been anticipating for more than half his life.

And she wouldn't even be around once Bobrzynyckolonycki was gone. How could he have let himself forget that?

"Willis, what's wrong?" she asked, her voice barely audible in the heavy silence that gripped the room.

"What's wrong?" he repeated evenly. "What's *wrong?*"

She nodded, but said nothing, clearly fearful of the tension that was fast thickening between them.

"I'll tell you what's wrong," he said as he made his way deliberately back to the bed. He bent and pounded each fist into the mattress, then fixed her with his gaze. "What's wrong is that last night was my best chance to study Bobrzynyckolonycki, and I blew it. I thoroughly *wasted* the entire night."

She paled when he said it, her fingers convulsing even tighter on the sheet. "You think last night was wasted?"

He expelled a restless breath of air, but his gaze never left hers. "What else would you call it? I wasn't at the telescope, where I *should* have been, and I wasn't doing what I should have been doing. I don't have one solitary observation, calculation, formulation or even speculation to offer for Bobrzynyckolonycki's movements last night, when it made its closest pass to the planet. I missed out completely on what should have been *the* most important night of my life."

She nodded, then rose silently and tugged the sheet from the bed, wrapping it around her like a sari. Willis bit back his urge to go over and peel it away from her again, to kiss her again, to make love to her again—and again, and again, and again. Instead, he simply watched her withdraw, fought back his disappointment and told himself it was for the better. She was going to withdraw from him one way or another anyhow. They might as well get it over with now.

"Gee, that's funny," she said, though there wasn't an ounce of humor in her voice or posture. "Because I went to sleep last night thinking it really *was* the most important night of *my* life."

He inhaled deeply at that, but had no idea what to say. He hadn't meant for the words that he had just spoken to be interpreted in the way she had obviously interpreted them. He'd simply uttered them without thinking, had let his anger at his own shortcomings overshadow his feelings for her. But then, that had always been his way of dealing with Rosemary March, he reminded himself: Don't think about the woman and the way she makes you feel. Think about preserving your sanity, instead.

"Last night didn't change anything with you, did it?" she asked.

Instead of answering her—something he simply could not allow himself to do—he posed a question of his own. "Why should last night have changed anything?"

She gaped at him, then emitted a soft, incredulous little gasp. "I should have known," she said softly.

"Known what?" he asked, not even trying to hide his irritation at the situation.

"I should have known that you had to make some kind of sacrifice so your body would be able to sustain that big brain of yours."

"And what, pray tell, would this sacrifice be?"

Instead of responding right away, she jerked the sheet completely from the bed and tossed the excess over her shoulder. Then, walking as if she'd been wounded, she made her way to the door. But she never explained her charge.

"Rosemary?" he called out as she gripped the knob, wondering why he bothered. Whatever supposed importance she placed on what had happened between them last night would evaporate the moment the comet passed outside its perceived circle of influence. As soon as Endicott breathed its collective sigh of relief that Bobrzynyckolonycki was beyond affecting them, Rosemary would go back to hating his guts. Why prolong the inevitable? he thought. Still, he had to know what she had meant by her cryptic statement.

"Rosemary?" he repeated when she didn't respond to his first summons.

She didn't turn around completely, but glanced back at him over her shoulder. "What?"

"What sacrifice?" he asked. "What did you mean?"

She dropped her gaze to the hand that held the doorknob, but her words were clearly meant for Willis. "In spite of how big you grew after high school," she told him, "I guess there just wasn't enough room for both of them inside you. You had to give one of them up."

"One of what?"

Now she lifted her gaze to study his face full on. "In order to make room for your brain, you obviously had to get rid of your heart. There just isn't enough room for both of them in there."

He knew that wasn't true the moment she said it, because he could feel his heart breaking. But before he could utter a word in denial, she tugged open the door and passed through it. Deep down, he wanted to call out after her. Deep down, he wanted to stop her. Deep down, he wanted to follow her and make love to her until she could see for herself how very wrong she was about him and his feelings for her.

But deep down, he knew that would be pointless. Because Bobrzynyckolonycki was officially on its way out now. The comet was fast leaving the earth and heading for the sun. And with every passing mile, the good citizens of Endicott would come closer to reclaiming their senses. In a matter of days, things would go back to normal. People would stop behaving strangely. The tourists would go home. The members of the scientific community would turn their studies to another phenomenon. And Rosemary March would go back to detesting him. Business as usual.

Dammit.

To punish himself for the grave sin of choosing love over science, Willis sentenced himself to solitary confinement in the attic for the remainder of his stay in Endicott. He and Rosemary returned to their initial practice of steadfastly avoiding each other, and the world seemed to go back to its normal rotation.

He still couldn't believe he had let happen what had happened. How could he have completely neglected his life's work during the single most important event of his studies? How could the simple desire to make love to Rosemary March have utterly usurped his need to understand and define something he'd been waiting more than half a lifetime to study? Because that's precisely what had happened that night. He'd forgotten all about Bob.

He groaned inwardly. Bob. In addition to everything else he'd done wrong, now he was actually referring to the comet by its common nickname. What scarcely a week ago had been the single most important scientific paradigm he'd ever encountered was suddenly nothing more than a really neato cosmic phenomenon that provided an excuse for an entire town to go temporarily bananas.

In spite of having missed Bobrzynyckolonycki's closest pass to the planet, he had thrown himself back into his research. He swung his gaze over to the big Random telescope that was aimed up at what would be a night sky in less than an hour. For the last five days, he had continued relentlessly with his studies on the outside chance that his research might still pan out. But so far, it hadn't. So far, Willis was as lacking in analysis and explanation for the comet's behavior as he had been when he was a thirteen-year-old novice. Bobrzynyckolonycki simply defied every effort he had made to analyze and explain.

Then something very strange had begun to happen. Gradually, over the last five days, his study of the comet had some-how begun to lose its appeal. And gradually, over the last five days, he had begun to wonder if his research had been what had spurred his return to Endicott at all.

Maybe it had actually been the prospect of seeing Rosemary again that had generated the little dance of heat in his belly when he'd discovered some weeks ago that he would be coming for the Comet Festival this year. Maybe it had actually been the prospect of winning Rosemary's respect—something he'd never had—that had inspired his relentless quest all these years to explain the unexplainable and land himself a spot in the annals of scientific discovery. Maybe it had actually been the slim possibility that the passage of fifteen years might have changed her feelings toward him that had been at the crux of this whole endeavor.

Because as each hour of each day had passed, as more time and space opened up between him and Rosemary, Willis had grown less and less interested in moving toward his telescope. Instead, he had wanted more and more to make his way down-stairs toward her. When all was said and done, it was as simple as that.

But there were a lot of people counting on him where this study was concerned, he had continuously reminded himself. A major university had invested a considerable amount of funding, time and trust in him and his project. To turn his back on all that would be unethical and unprofessional. He still had a few precious days to try to make sense of Bobrzyny-ckolonycki. Even if he felt pretty hopeless about ever mending the rift between him and Rosemary.

But instead of forcing himself to his feet and crossing the room to his telescope, notes, charts and research, he sat on the floor on the other side of the attic, staring out the window at the stain of the pink sunset painting the sky. And he worried that in a matter of days, he would be packing up his things and going home. Back to Cambridge, back to MIT, back to his studies, his classroom and his observatory. Back to all the things he needed to exercise his mind and make himself feel alive.

Back where he would be alone again, with nothing to keep him company but a great big brain, brimming with regrets.

Willis braced his elbows on his knees, buried his head in his hands and wondered how on earth he was going to make up for his egregious transgressions of falling in love with Rosemary March and failing to understand Bobrzynyckolonycki. But one thought greatly overshadowed the other, and memories of Rosemary filled his brain. Memories of how incredible it had been to make love with her. Of how right and good and natural it had felt to hold her and be held by her. Of how he wanted nothing more for the rest of his life than to spend it with her, doing things like that.

He sighed heavily, fancying that he could feel his brain beginning to deteriorate already. The promise of eternal carnal satisfaction was calling to him much more loudly than the considerably more noble perpetual quest for knowledge. Truth be told, Bobrzynyckolonycki or no Bobrzynyckolonycki, there was probably still time for him to straighten things out with Rosemary, maybe even to the point where the two of them could share some kind of future together. But what kind of future would it be when neither of them shared even the most basic common trait?

Beauty or brains. His libido or his cerebrum. If Willis could only choose one or the other, what would his choice be? And by posing such a question of himself, wasn't he guilty of the most heinous superficiality? Perhaps, unconsciously, he'd already made his selection. But was it the right one?

For an intelligent, intellectual man, one who had spent his adult life performing research, he was suddenly all out of answers, and had no idea how to go about finding more.

His gaze fell on the boxes of Rosemary's belongings, items that had provided him with an occasional distraction during the long nights he had spent in the attic waiting for something to happen out in the cosmos. He'd practically memorized her collection of Endicott Central High School yearbooks by now. And he'd perused a number of her class notebooks from which actual class notes had been glaringly absent. Instead, the pages had been filled with doodles and scribbles, unfinished notes to

Angie and Kirby and a few odd sketches of landscapes, animals and people, illustrations that had shown remarkable skill for one so young.

It was for one of those notebooks that Willis reached now, in the hope of finding at least a temporary distraction, something to take his mind off the troubling thoughts that assailed him. Something to kill some time until darkness descended, when he could see if he had any hope in hell of salvaging something from his studies of Bobrzynyckolonycki. The spiral-bound notebook had a dark-green cover, upon which was inscribed in a loopy, feminine hand the words *Rosemary March* and *Chemistry*.

Oh, boy, Willis thought dryly. Rosemary's notebook from chemistry class. This ought to be good for a laugh.

He flipped it open to find what he had found in all the others, page after page of doodling, drawing and sketching, and nary an equation or logarithm in the bunch. He shook his head. There was the odd—odd because it was correct—notation of something their chemistry teacher, Mrs. Dumont, had doubtless written on the blackboard, a reference to the periodic table—much of which was misspelled—and an aborted attempt at figuring out the atomic weight of boron.

And among all that, a note begun but never delivered to Kirby: *Dear Kirb, W. is driving me NUTS! I don't know how much longer I can take this...* The "W." in question was doubtless he himself, he thought. Until he read further. *There are times when I wish I could tell him how much I love him. But I don't think he'd believe me. If I told YOU, you wouldn't believe me, either. I don't think ANYONE would believe me....*

The "W." she was writing about was Walt Zapfel, Willis realized as a knot tightened his belly. Then he noted the date on the missive. November 1. Rosemary hadn't started going out with Walt until the spring. She'd always dated guys according to the sport indigenous to that particular season. During football season, she would have been going out with Chuck Woods, the quarterback for the Yellowjackets. A lot of people had called him Woody, Rosemary, evidently, among them. Willis frowned. Jeez, she'd actually been in love with that jerk?

He shook his head and tossed the notebook back into the box, then sorted through the few remainders. At the very bottom of the box, he uncovered a sketch pad of heavy, white vellum paper. It, too, was filled with remarkably good work—watercolor paintings this time, instead of pencil drawings. As he flipped through the pages, Willis realized the pictures constructed a story of sorts. And tucked into the back, some pages torn from a spiral notebook that were folded in half, as if hidden there.

He unfolded them and read, and as he read, he smiled. The pages were undated, but appeared to be several years old. Rosemary had written a children's story to go along with the softly colored illustrations, a story about a little girl who refused to go to bed. So she followed the course of the sun to the west, knowing that as long as it never set, bedtime would never come. And in her travels, she visited a variety of exotic locales, from Abu Dhabi to Zanzibar. A geography lesson for young minds, disguised as entertainment.

Willis frowned as he considered the import of what he held in his hands. A geography lesson. An accurate one, too. If this particular project was any indication, Rosemary March knew her geography backward and forward. And wasn't geography a *science?*

He stuffed the notebook pages back into the sketchbook, slammed it shut and tossed it quickly back into the box. So she'd pulled out an atlas and done some research, he thought. Big deal. That didn't mean anything. Still, he wondered why she hadn't pursued her artistic abilities. She was obviously very talented. Why hadn't she carried her art studies further?

The front door slammed downstairs, announcing Rosemary's return, and Willis turned his gaze back to the open window. Outside, the sun was dropping lower toward the horizon, streaking the sky with pink and yellow and orange in preparation for its full departure. The sun was going down, taking its warmth and brightness with it. But Rosemary had come home.

He heard her scaling the stairs with a staccato pace, but instead of staying where he was, as he had for the last five days upon her return home, he went to the hole in the floor of the attic to wait for her appearance below. When she topped the last stair, she glanced up at the attic door and saw him looking down at her before he said a word in summons. The cotton tank dress she wore was much the color of the orangey sky outside, and something inside Willis warmed at the sight of her.

For one long moment, they only stood there staring at each other, and he wished he knew what she was thinking about. She looked hurt. Anxious. Lonely. Pretty much the way he was feeling inside.

Suddenly feeling weak for some reason, and not sure his legs would hold him much longer, he dropped down onto his haunches and let his hands dangle between his knees. "Can we talk?" he asked softly, uncertain when he'd decided to pose the question.

She dropped her gaze to the floor. "I don't think we have anything to talk about."

"I do."

She glanced back up at that, but her expression was cautious, untrusting. "Then talk."

"Could you come up here?"

"Why don't you come down here?"

He hesitated, then thrust a thumb over his shoulder, toward the window. "There's a beautiful sunset coming. You don't want to miss it."

She inhaled deeply, then seemed to surrender. "Let me just put my purse in my room."

He nodded, then rose and moved away from the entry. After a few minutes, he heard her climbing up the stairs, then her head poked through the floor, followed by the rest of her. Once again, her startling beauty struck him, stirring him in places deep down inside himself that he hadn't even realized could feel. And he wondered why that couldn't be enough for him.

She stepped out onto the floor of the attic, then strode to the window that wasn't obscured by his telescope. The way the soft light washed over her, he was reminded of the water-color paintings in her sketchbook, the pinks and yellows and corals that swirled and danced on the page. And he was over-come by so much confusion, he scarcely knew where to begin.

"Okay," she said quietly, staring out at the dying sunlight. "I'm listening."

He expelled a restless breath and ran a big hand awkwardly through his hair. "And suddenly, I have no idea what to say."

She turned to look at him. "That's funny. Suddenly I can think of a lot of things I'd like to say."

"Such as?"

She shook her head and returned her attention to the sky outside. "Nothing I say to you will ever make any differ-ence."

"Why won't it?"

She turned to look at him again, crossing her arms defen-sively over her chest. Her dark eyes were bright with what he didn't want to think were tears. Unfortunately, he was fairly certain that they were.

"Because, Willis," she said, stumbling a bit over his name, "you have set ideas about the universe and everything in it that are never going to change, no matter what. That's why."

"That's not true."

"Of course it's true."

"No, it isn't." Feeling edgy, he began to pace, unheedful of the fact that his movements brought him closer and closer to Rosemary every time he began a new circuit. "If I had constant, preconceived notions about the universe," he said, "then I wouldn't be here trying to understand Bobrzynycko-lonycki."

She noted his gradual approach, but didn't try to move out of his way. "Yeah, well, maybe you're trying to understand the wrong thing. Did you ever think about that?"

He halted abruptly and met her gaze levelly. "Not until recently."

She expelled an errant breath of air. "What's that supposed to mean?"

This time he was the one to shake his head. "Nothing. Never mind."

"You don't think I'd understand."

"No," he agreed. "I don't think you would."

She nodded, her eyes growing darker. "Because I'm too stupid."

"No," he was quick to contradict her. "I don't think you'd understand it, because I'm not sure even *I* understand it."

"And of course, if the brilliant Dr. Willis Random, with his five college degrees, can't understand it, then certainly stupid little Rosemary March, who flunked out of community college and beauty school, doesn't have a hope of figuring it out, either."

"That wasn't what I meant."

"Oh, wasn't it."

Again, she had uttered the remark not as a question, but as a statement. However, unlike before, this time, Willis *could* contradict her. "No. It wasn't."

"Then what did you mean?"

He hesitated for another moment, wondering if he really wanted to do what he was about to do, to pose the question he really wanted to pose. Without further consideration, however, he said, "Can I ask you a question?"

She lifted one shoulder, then let it drop, but her anxious expression belied the casualness of the gesture. "I guess so."

He eyed her intently, telling himself he was crazy for asking. Nevertheless, the question taunted him, and he knew he couldn't leave things the way they were between them. He had to know for sure. He had to ask her outright. Otherwise, he might never know another decent night's sleep in his life. So he took a deep breath and forced the words out of his mouth.

"Rosemary," he began slowly, "there's something very important I need to know."

She swallowed visibly, her expression turning somber. "Okay. What?"

Willis inhaled deeply, met her gaze levelly and asked as evenly, as clearly, as he could, "What's the capital of Albania?"

Ten

Rosemary chuckled nervously, glancing first to the right and then to the left, wondering for a moment if she was being secretly surveilled by hidden cameras. Then she realized she must have misheard Willis's question. "What?" she asked, hoping for some clarification.

But he only continued to study her gravely as he repeated exactly what she had thought she'd heard him say the first time. "What's the capital of Albania?" he asked again.

She hesitated, still waiting for the punch line, for some kind of elaboration, for Allen Funt to come popping out from behind the telescope and tell her to smile because she was on *Candid Camera*. When none of those things happened, she returned her attention to Willis and asked, "What does that have to do with anything?"

"I just want to know. Tell me. What's the capital of Albania?"

Surrendering to the inquiry, she replied automatically, "Tirana. Why?"

"How about Burma? What's the capital of Burma?"

She hesitated again, eyeing him warily, waiting to see what kind of joke he was playing on her. Finally, evidently deciding he was serious—and curious herself to know exactly where this line of questioning was going—she told him, "Actually, it's not called Burma anymore. It's called Myanmar."

"What's the capital?" he repeated.

"Yangon."

"How about Botswana?"

"The capital of Botswana?" she asked.

He nodded.

"Gaborone."

"Yemen?"

"Sanaa."

"Mauritania?"

"Nouakchott."

Rosemary watched Willis closely as he took a few steps backward and seated himself on one of the many boxes stacked nearby. For a moment, he only sat there staring at her, his fingers steepled in front of his mouth, his elbows perched on his knees. She shook her head, still confused, wishing she knew what was going on.

"Willis?" she asked anxiously. "What's with the geography lesson?"

He dropped his hands down between his legs, keeping his fingers linked loosely. But he continued to survey her. "You, uh…you seem to know a lot about geography."

She shrugged off the observation. "I've always been interested in geography. Foreign places. Exotic locales. It's one of the reasons I became a travel agent."

"But you seem to know all kinds of obscure things about geography."

She shook her head. "Those weren't obscure things. Everybody knows the capital of Mauritania is Nouakchott."

He laughed a little nervously. "Everybody knows that? Rosemary, I don't think anyone who lives more than a hundred miles outside Mauritania knows that. *I* certainly didn't know it."

"You didn't?"

He shook his head slowly. "I've never heard of any of those places you just rolled off. Hell, I didn't even know Burma wasn't Burma anymore."

She chuckled a little anxiously, but felt in no way amused. "Sure you did."

"No, I didn't."

She stared at him for a moment, processing that little bit of information. "Are you saying that I know something you don't know?"

He nodded, his mouth twisting grudgingly into a tight little smile. "Apparently, you know something a lot of people don't know. You seem to know a lot of things that *I* don't know."

She should have felt vindicated, she told herself. Instead, she just felt more confused than ever. "But I thought you knew everything," she said softly.

His smile fell, his expression turning melancholy. He inhaled heavily, releasing the breath in a whispery, ragged rush of air. His voice was so quiet she almost didn't hear him when he said, "So did I. Clearly I was wrong about that, too."

Rosemary shook her head slowly, her confusion compounding. "Willis, I don't understand what any of this has to do with...with us. You and me, I mean. Isn't that what you wanted to talk about in the first place?"

He stood, settling his hands restively on his hips. "I thought we were talking about us...about you and me."

"What does the capital of Albania—or Mauritania, for that matter—have to do with you and me?"

"More than you know," he told her cryptically.

She narrowed her eyes and shook her head again. "I still don't know what you mean."

"I mean that for a guy who's purported to be such a profound thinker, I have a lot to learn." The words were spoken with obvious reluctance, as if he hated admitting that more than anything else in the world, to Rosemary above all people.

She told herself she should feel optimistic about his statement, but something hanging heavy and cold inside her lingered. There was something in Willis's voice, in his posture, in his eyes, that suggested there was a lot more going on with him right now than a simple confrontation with his alleged superiority in the intelligence department. The way he was looking at her was almost pained somehow. As if it hurt him just to be in the same room with her.

Instead of dwelling on that, however, Rosemary tried to make light of the situation, in spite of the miserable way she felt inside. "Some genius you are," she told him quietly, forcing a smile that didn't even feel convincing. "I could have told you that a long time ago."

She turned to go, thinking the conversation he'd requested was over, despite the fact that they seemed to have said or settled nothing at all.

"Wait, Rosemary," he said, sounding suddenly hurried, concerned.

She turned to find him bending over one of the many cardboard boxes that had been storing her youth and childhood since she had moved into her grandmother's house. When he straightened, he was holding on to a sketchbook, one of many she supposed were stashed up here in the attic somewhere. There had been a time in her life when sketching and painting had provided her with an enjoyable pastime. For a while, she had even thought about pursuing her art professionally. But somewhere along the way, she had abandoned those dreams. She couldn't remember why now.

"I need to ask you something else," Willis said as he flipped to the back of the sketchbook and withdrew a sheaf of notebook papers.

Despite the turmoil that had beset her that day, she smiled when she realized what it was and took a few steps forward. "Oh, wow, I'd forgotten about that."

She reached out and took the sketchbook from Willis, and flipped idly through the pages. But she said nothing as she shook her head in wonder at what the artwork housed there represented.

"It, uh…it looks like illustrations and the story line for a children's book," Willis said.

She glanced up to see him studying not the pages in his hand, but her face. "It is," she confessed. "I designed this…gosh, I guess about nine or ten years ago. After I dropped out of beauty school.''

"Did you ever send it out to any publishers?"

She made a wry face. "Oh, God, no. Why would I do something like that?''

A soft smile curled his lips. "Just a shot in the dark here, but maybe to sell it and start a career in the children's book market?''

Rosemary snatched the papers from his hands and stuffed them into the back of the sketchbook, snapped it shut tight and tossed it back down into the box. "Oh, right. Like I have the talent for something like that.''

"You don't think you do?

She shrugged off the question. "No.''

"Why not?''

She gaped at him. "Oh, come on, Willis. You, above all people, know better than to ask a question like that.''

He eyed her back, his expression a mixture of puzzlement and concern. "Why me, above all people?''

She shook her head at him, her mouth still hanging open in disbelief. "Because you know better than anyone what a lack of ability I have for anything like that.''

He snapped his mouth shut and said nothing, only stared at her in total silence. Rosemary took it as a confirmation of the statement she had just uttered, not that she needed confirmation for that. Not from Willis, anyway. She already knew what his opinion of her mental capabilities were. She ought to be grateful he *wasn't* saying anything.

"What have you been doing up here, going through my things?'' she asked, diverting the attention from herself to him. "This stuff is kind of personal, Willis. You could have asked first.''

"I'm sorry," he apologized, the words automatic, flat. "I noticed the yearbooks one night when nothing much was going on up in the sky, and picked one up. After that, it turned into something of a habit, I suppose.''

"And you started prying into my personal stuff," she reiterated.

He nodded. "I suppose I did. I apologize."

She inhaled softly and lifted a hand to her forehead, where a throbbing pain had erupted out of nowhere. "It doesn't matter," she said. Though deep down, in the very darkest, most secret parts of her heart, it did. It mattered a lot. She couldn't remember what was in those boxes, and frankly, she just didn't want Willis having knowledge of anything personal about her.

Kind of late for that, isn't it? a voice in her head taunted. *Hey, after what happened last weekend...*

What happened last weekend meant nothing, she assured the voice, knowing she was lying even as the thought materialized. Nevertheless, she had to concede that there was some inkling of truth in the realization. Where Willis was concerned, at least, what had happened between them the weekend before clearly had meant nothing.

"Just leave my stuff alone, okay?" she warned him. "Leave *me* alone."

"But, Rosemary—"

"We don't have anything more to say to each other," she told him, turning toward the attic's exit. "I think everything you said Sunday morning after we..." She cut herself off before she could put voice to what had happened and make it seem more real. "Everything you said Sunday morning," she continued quietly, "pretty much let me know how things are between us. You care more about your studies and research than anything else in the world. And I care more about—"

She stopped herself just in time, before she confessed that she cared more about Willis than anything else in the world. That she'd felt that way for half her life. That she would doubtless continue to feel that way for all the years she had left. Last weekend had meant nothing? she taunted herself ruthlessly. Hey, last weekend had meant *everything* to her. She would never be able to forget about Willis now.

"You care more about what?"

His question came softly from behind her, and before she did something really stupid like answer him with the truth, Rosemary dove for the hole in the attic floor and hurried down the steps. She nearly stumbled on the rickety rungs more than once, but righted herself each time before she fell. Fell face first onto the hallway floor, anyway.

Unfortunately, there was nothing she could do about having fallen in love with Willis. Something inside told her that wasn't likely to change. Ever.

Willis didn't follow her, because he was too busy trying to fight off the incessant buzzing that had overtaken his brain, causing the complete malfunctioning of every last one of his motor skills. Mainly because it was punctuated by Rosemary's voice rumbling through his mind over and over again.

You know better than anyone what a lack of ability I have...

Because I'm too stupid...

Hey, I'm just a simpleminded, slack-brained know-nothing, after all...

His knees buckled beneath him, and he collapsed back down onto the cardboard box he had used as a seat before. Then he covered the lower half of his face with his hands and stared blindly out at the attic. She had only been repeating things he had said about her himself. Sometimes out loud to her face, sometimes silently to himself. But they had all originated with him.

Willis *had* always considered Rosemary to be of below-average intelligence. He had never once considered the possibility that she might have some talent or proficiency that she kept hidden from the rest of the world. He had simply assumed that because she was gorgeous and sexy and couldn't understand the scientific concepts he grasped so effortlessly, then she must not be able to understand anything at all.

And just *why* had she kept her artistic talent and proficiency in geography hidden? he asked himself. Because Willis Random had made her feel like a useless moron who couldn't possibly have anything to offer anyone, that's why.

A lead weight settled in his belly as he realized that he was responsible for preventing Rosemary from reaching her potential. He was responsible for preventing her from following a dream. For preventing her from exploring her abilities and talents to their fullest measure.

Because he'd known she hadn't liked him, and with a few careless words, Willis had struck blows that had gone so deep Rosemary had never recovered from them. She had carried them into adulthood, had let them stain her perception of herself to this day.

And as if all that wasn't bad enough, he mused further, growing ever sicker inside, his attacks hadn't even had foundation. She wasn't an empty, beautiful shell with nothing to offer. On the contrary, she had the talent and smarts and personality to potentially touch a lot of lives. A lot of young lives. A lot of young, impressionable lives.

If she pursued a career writing and illustrating books for children—and even with his limited knowledge of such things, Willis was convinced she would indeed be successful in such an endeavor—then she could contribute to the literacy and artistic sensibilities of an entire generation. Of the future generations spawned by that generation. She could teach children things. Fertilize their imaginations. Exercise their minds. And her influence could conceivably go on indefinitely.

Hell, Willis thought, shaken by the realization, if she put her mind to it, Rosemary March had it in her to virtually change the world someday. Where he himself, *if* he was lucky, might potentially figure out the comings and goings of a comet someday.

Big deal. To put it in layman's terms.

He hung his head in his hands completely, curling his fists in his hair. Could this possibly get any worse than it already was? Was there any way to feel more guilty than he already did about how he had treated Rosemary?

From his vantage point, his gaze fell back on the box into which she had discarded her sketchbook. Beside it was a red notebook that caught his eye, mainly because it bore no marks of identification. Not sure why he did it, Willis reached for it and began to flip through it. More sketches in number two pencil—many of them remarkably good. And along with the artwork, dated entries of prose. Page after page after page.

At first he thought it was another story she had written, and he began to read. Immediately, however, he realized what he was holding in his hand was a journal from Rosemary's high school years—her adolescent observations, her teenage thoughts, her youthful dreams and desires. And even though he knew it would be a violation of privacy to read the words she'd recorded, even though she'd just told him to leave her stuff alone, Willis found that he simply couldn't help himself:

10/23/84. School was horrible today. I'm not sure how much longer I can do this. I wish W. could see how much I love him. I wish I could tell him. I see him at school, and I can hardly believe it myself that I feel the way I do about him. If anyone else found out, especially W., I'd never live it down....

Great, he thought. More about Chuck Woods, quarterback. He skimmed ahead, knowing guiltily that deep down, he was hoping there would be some mention of himself in the journal, knowing he was only going to be disappointed, instead. Nevertheless, he read on:

12/20/84. Finally. Christmas vacation. I've had it with school. I need a break. W. still doesn't know how I feel about him, and sometimes I get so close to breaking down and just yelling out "I LOVE YOU!" that I can't stand it....

Something was wrong. Willis detected it right away. December was basketball season. And during basketball season, Rosemary had dated Leo McCauley, Yellowjackets center. So why was she still going on about W.? Was she carrying a torch for Woody? Starting to pine for Walt? Willis read some more:

But it would be so stupid for me to tell him how much I love him. He'll never love me back. He could never love a simpleminded, slack-brained know-nothing like me. And that's exactly what he calls me, all the time....

A fire exploded in his belly as he read the words. Twice, because he didn't trust his eyes the first time. Surely they didn't say what he understood them to say. Surely the *W.* in Rosemary's journal didn't stand for…*Willis.* Did it? His heart rate doubling, he hastily thumbed ahead a few more pages:

In chemistry today, we made soap. Or at least, we tried to. W. knew what he was doing, but I, of course, idiot that I am, totally screwed it up. Mrs. Dumont gave us a C, and W. about hit the roof, saying he'd never get into MIT now. But even with him mad at me, I still love him. I wish I were smarter. I wish he could like me just a little bit….

He ruffled ahead through the pages, toward the end of the journal:

Graduation day. It feels so weird. On one hand, I'm so happy to be done with school. But leaving Endicott Central means I'll never see W. again. He's off to MIT, to greater things that will never include someone like me. I wish I could go with him. I can just hear everyone laughing at that. Stupid Rosemary March applying to MIT. What a joke. They'd laugh even harder if they knew the reason I want to go is to be close to W., even if I am way too dumb for him to ever love me.

But it's BECAUSE W. is so smart that I love him so much. There's just something so sexy about that much intelligence. Sometimes, when he talks about stuff in chemistry, stuff I don't even understand, I just get so TURNED ON. I don't care if he does look like a pizza-faced little twerp. There's more to people than their looks. Lots more. And even if W. thinks I have the IQ of a lint brush, I know I'll never forget him….

His mouth was dry, his T-shirt damp with sweat when he looked up again. His vision blurred, his focus directed fifteen years into the past. Rosemary March had loved him when they were in high school. She had actually loved him. As deeply as a fifteen-year-old girl could love. And it had lasted far beyond the appearance and disappearance of a comet, until the day they'd graduated from high school. Willis couldn't blame this one on Bobrzynyckolonycki.

Rosemary had loved him, he marveled again. Him. A thirteen-year-old geek with braces and broken glasses and a face only a mother could love. A mother and, evidently, a fifteen-year-old sexpot who could have had her pick of the boys at school. A girl who had referred to herself in her own journal as "stupid," "dumb" and a "simpleminded, slack-brained know-nothing," because that's how Willis had made her feel.

There's more to people than their looks. Lots more....

Oh, boy. Hadn't he learned that the hard way himself, a long, long time ago. But Rosemary had seen beyond his physical shell and had fallen for what was beneath it. His brain. His superior brain. The brain he'd always considered so far above everyone else's.

And he'd been too stupid to realize that a warm, wonderful, intelligent, beautiful girl was in love with him.

Could she still love him now? he wondered. Had that been what was actually going on all along since his return to Endicott? Could Rosemary still be in love with him after all these years? Even after the things he'd said and done to her? Even after he'd behaved like such a simpleminded, slack-brained know-nothing?

He shook his head slowly, sighed heavily at the silence and wondered how on earth he could ever have imagined himself an intelligent man, and what he was going to have to do to win Rosemary back.

Eleven

Six days after it had happened, Rosemary still couldn't quite believe she'd made love with Willis. At times, she could almost convince herself it had been a dream, because the perfection of the moment, the exquisiteness of her emotions, the utter joy that had overcome her that night simply seemed too wonderful to have been real.

Then she would recall the warmth and strength of his bare back as she'd dug her fingertips into his shoulder blades, would remember the musky scent of him that had surrounded her as he'd claimed her body with his, would experience again the explosion of heat that had rocked her when they'd climaxed as one. And she would know full well that it had truly happened.

And that it would never happen again.

She sighed heavily and stared blindly at the computer terminal on her desk at Jet-Set Travels. Now that the Comet Festival was winding up, Endicott was settling down, returning to its regular, quiet pace. And with autumn fast approaching, there wasn't a lot of work to keep a travel agent's mind oc-

cupied. Which had left Rosemary lots of time for daydreaming, whether she liked it or not. And daydreaming meant that
her thoughts inevitably circled back to Willis.

Briefly, she'd embraced some small hope that things might
work out between them. The morning after they made love,
when she realized that in the heat of the moment, they'd done
nothing to protect themselves from the repercussions of their
actions, she had actually found herself hoping she would become pregnant as a result.

A part of her hoped that still.

Though why she would want to put herself through the or-
deal of single parenting, she couldn't have said. A baby would
just be a constant reminder of how badly things had gone
wrong with Willis. But a baby would also mean that she
wouldn't have to spend the rest of her life alone.

She'd seen nothing of Willis that week until yesterday afternoon, when they'd shared a lesson in geography, a lesson
in art and a lesson in futility. She supposed he was working
twice as hard as normal to make up for missing the comet's
peak performance Saturday night. Certainly she had heard his
movements overhead from time to time, as she had lain in bed
awake, wondering how things between the two of them might
have been different. But invariably, by the time she rose for
work in the morning Willis had gone to bed. And by the time
she came home at night he had banished himself to the attic.

So except for yesterday, she hadn't even had the privilege
of gazing upon him to satisfy her longings. Instead, she'd been
forced to make do with her memories. Might as well get used
to it, she told herself. Because that was sure to be the pattern
of her life from now on.

She turned her attention back to the computer screen, but
she let her gaze ricochet from one column of information to
another, without taking note of anything. There was nothing
pressing she needed to do today, and with three other agents
in the office, there was no reason for her to hang around.

She thought momentarily about calling her two best friends,
to see if they wanted to play hooky with her, then dismissed
the idea at once. Kirby was too hard at work trying to ruin

her good reputation around town with that bad boy James Nash, and Angie was wallowing in self-pity now that her new husband had left her. Neither of them would have been in any shape to cheer Rosemary up.

She glanced over at her co-workers. "Anybody mind if I cut out early?" she asked.

The three women shook their heads, one murmuring that it was Rosemary's turn to take off early anyway. She smiled, offered her thanks, then collected her things and headed for the door.

When she pulled into her driveway, the first thing she noticed were the two cats stretched out to receive maximum sunlight on the sidewalk leading to the front porch. She shook her head at the sight, but couldn't help smiling. Why couldn't she and Willis have gotten along as well as their cats did? Then again, she supposed, a cat wasn't overly preoccupied by what its potential mate was carrying in its cranial cavity. When it came to mating, cats were driven by more primitive, more natural, behavior.

Rosemary remembered again the way she and Willis had turned to each other that night, then grew warm and wanton all over again recalling the ways he had touched her, both inside and out. And she decided pretty quickly that there was a lot to be said for primitive behavior.

"Hi, Ska. Hi, Ice," she greeted the animals as she strode by them, out of habit reducing the big white cat's big long name to a moniker that seemed much more appropriate.

Each of the animals twitched a paw in greeting, but otherwise didn't alter their prime sunbathing postures. Rosemary couldn't help but smile. Then she wondered if Ska would be as lonely as she would be once Willis packed up all his belongings—including his cat—and returned to Cambridge.

She stooped to rub her hand affectionately over Ska's soft, mottled belly. "Looks like it'll be back to me and you and the zombies of Mora Tau once Willis leaves," she murmured. "Oh, well. Maybe Ice will send you some postcards from Massachusetts. I'll do my best to read them to you, though if he's like his master, his vocabulary is probably light-years bigger than mine.''

Ska opened one eye and surveyed her mistress dubiously, as if to say, *Who, him? Don't sweat it. He's not nearly as smart as he looks.*

After one final brush of her hand over each of the animals, Rosemary stood and made her way toward the house. She shivered involuntarily against the cool breeze that swept over the bare arms left unprotected by her short-sleeved uniform shirt. The balmy Indian-summer days Endicott had been enjoying were gradually growing more appropriate for autumn. She hastened her step as she approached the porch, then halted suddenly when she realized Willis was standing at the door waiting for her.

''Hi,'' he said casually through the screen, as if greeting her warmly upon her return home from work were something he did every afternoon.

''Hi,'' she replied automatically.

He pushed the door outward in invitation, and once more, a ripple of familiarity washed over her, as if this, too, were something utterly natural in their relationship.

''How was your day?'' he asked.

She narrowed her eyes at him. ''Fine.''

''You're home early.''

''Ye-ess....''

She stretched the word out over several zip codes, not sure exactly why he was behaving this way. As if he were happy to see her. As if sharing this little welcome-home ritual was just that—a ritual. As if he were important in her life. As if she were important in his.

''Well, come on in,'' he told her, stepping aside enough for her to pass by him.

But not enough for her to pass by without touching him.

She hesitated for a moment, then decided she was being silly. Willis was simply trying to be polite, that was all. And considering the way they'd parted four days earlier, it was the least he could do. He'd be returning to Cambridge in a matter of days, and there was no reason they shouldn't at least be courteous to each other in the meantime. Courtesy, she repeated to herself. That was all that was at the root of their relationship now.

But when she stepped over the threshold, instead of moving courteously out of her way, Willis seemed to move closer. Her shoulder grazed his chest, and even with that slight touch, she fancied she could feel the heat of his body penetrating hers. An echo of longing whispered through her, but she ignored it, ruthlessly reminding herself that Willis didn't want her. Not with a deep, binding emotion that overruled everything else in his life. Not the way she wanted him. Although he might admit to a certain physical attraction, it was only knowledge and intellect that would satisfy his needs. And she was supremely lacking in both.

"Supper won't be ready for another couple of hours," he announced offhandedly as she cleared the foyer.

She spun around to gaze at him, her eyebrows arched in surprise. "You're cooking supper?" she asked.

He nodded, again with that kind of matter-of-factness that suggested she shouldn't be surprised by the news.

"Why?" she asked him.

"Special occasion," he replied.

She eyed him suspiciously. "What's the occasion? Did you figure out the elusive Comet Bob?"

He shook his head, but seemed in no way bothered by that development. "No. I haven't even come close to understanding the comet. In fact, you might say I'm more confused than ever. *But…*" He smiled as he uttered the simple conjunction. "I've made a much more significant discovery. One that is bound to change lives irrevocably."

Her heart sank at the announcement. Now he'd never stop using his brain long enough to enjoy simpler pursuits. Not that she'd expected him to in the first place. Still, she realized that a big part of her had been hoping for some small miracle along those lines—that Willis might, for even a moment, feel instead of think. She was sure he would like it if he'd just give it a chance.

"What did you discover?" she asked halfheartedly.

He watched her thoughtfully for a moment, then told her, "We can talk about it after you change."

"Why can't we talk about it now?"

"Oh, it can wait a little while," he said with a soft smile. "I imagine you want to get out of your work clothes." Then, out of nowhere, his smile went from playful to predatory. "Although I think there's something profoundly arousing about that little outfit."

A quick explosion ignited in Rosemary's belly, spreading heat outward at an alarming rate. "Wh-what's that supposed to mean?" she stammered.

He shrugged, as if his statement had held no more significance than a bingo call. "Just that I've passed many a night up in the attic fantasizing about what you might have on under that conservative little navy blue skirt and starched white blouse, that's all."

Her mouth dropped open in astonishment. "What?"

He nodded thoughtfully, his expression turning a little dreamy. "Yeah," he began with a wistful little note of longing tinting his voice, "whenever I got tired of looking at galaxies and nebulae, my mind would start wandering to thoughts about you and your work uniform...and what you might—or might not—be wearing underneath it...and what it would be like to have you come home, and have one thing lead to another, and..." His predator's smile returned. "Well, let's just say that for a man of science, lately I've had a pretty active fantasy life."

Rosemary swallowed hard. "I think maybe you've been working too hard."

He nodded. "I think maybe you're right."

"You do?"

He nodded again, this time following up the gesture with a step toward her. Then another, and another, and another, until there was no room for him to take anymore. Then he settled his hands on her hips and pulled her toward him, effectively closing the negligible distance left between them.

"Just what do you think you're doing?" she asked him, the question coming out breathless because she had forgotten to breathe. She doubled her fists loosely against his chest, when what she really wanted to do was splay them open over his heart.

"I'm *not* thinking," he told her. "That's the point. I'm taking the night off from thinking. I'm going to spend it doing instead."

She was almost afraid to ask, but said carefully, "Doing what?"

He hesitated only a moment before telling her, "Making love to the woman who loves me."

Her eyes widened at that, and she willed herself not to panic. Instead, she swallowed hard and tried to bluff. "Well, gee, Willis, don't you think that woman's going to get a bit miffed that you've got your arms around me?"

He shook his head and smiled again. "Not a chance." He pressed his fingers more intimately into her hips, then bent to touch his forehead to her own. "Come on, Rosemary. Admit it. You love me."

She covered his hands with her own, but instead of prying them loose from her hips, she simply stood there and enjoyed the feel of their rough, warm texture. When she curled her fingers around his wrists, she detected the rush of his pulse beneath her fingertips. And only then did she realize that he was nowhere near as cool and collected as he was letting on. Willis was nervous. Maybe even a little scared. Of her. How very strange.

"Willis?" she said, her voice barely a whisper.

"Yes?"

"What makes you so sure that I love you?"

His throat worked over a swallow with some difficulty, and he lifted a hand to her hair, winding a dark curl around his index finger. Then, very softly, he said, "I have it in writing."

Something hot splashed in her belly, heating her insides, the fire spreading quickly throughout her body. "Oh?" she asked. "I don't remember signing anything to that effect."

He smiled a little nervously. "Don't you? Then come upstairs with me. There's something I need to show you."

Rosemary's rational mind told her she'd be foolish to follow him anywhere, that going with Willis would lead to nothing but heartache. But her heart ached to follow him nonetheless, to spend even a few more minutes in the same room with him, regardless of how he felt about her. If such a thing meant she was stupid, well, then she was indeed everything he had ever accused her of being. But she couldn't help how she felt. She couldn't help it if she loved Willis. And she couldn't help it if he didn't love her in return.

No matter.

What mattered was that this might be her last chance to spend time with him, to be close to him, to talk to him. In a few days, he'd be driving back home across a half-dozen states, and she might never see him again. There was no reason to waste time wishing she could be more and he could want less. There was only now, and she'd be stupid not to take advantage of it.

"Okay," she agreed as something twisted inside her.

Without another word, he wove his fingers with hers and led her toward the stairs. Neither of them spoke until they reached the top, where Rosemary staggered a bit when she started to move toward the attic steps, and Willis took a step toward his bedroom.

"I thought we were going up to the attic," she said.

He shook his head. "In here."

He gave her hand a gentle tug, drawing her into the guest bedroom he had occupied since his arrival—the room she had visited only once since then, for one long, delirious night of lovemaking that would have to satisfy her for the rest of her life. And even though that night had changed her completely and irretrievably, the room itself seemed not to have changed at all. Still painted pale yellow, still furnished with the bird's-eye maple pieces her grandmother had owned, still touched with flowered chintz accessories, it was far too feminine a room for such a masculine, dominating man.

No wonder he'd spent so much time in the attic, she thought. Well, aside from the fact that he'd wanted as little to do with her as possible, of course.

Then she noted that there was indeed something different

in the room, something that hadn't been there before, something that didn't belong there at all. Two things, in fact. The sketchbook Willis had uncovered the day before, the one holding the children's story she'd designed so many years ago. And beside it, a red spiral notebook whose identity she only now remembered. She'd always color-coded her notebooks when she was a teenager. Blue for history. Green for science. Yellow for math. White for English.

And red for things that spilled from the heart. Like the notebook that lay so casually on Willis's bed.

"What are you doing with one of my journals?" she asked as something tightened in her chest.

She crossed the room and snatched it up, clutching it fiercely to her heart, as if that could protect the fragile thoughts and dreams and wishes she had penned within. She spun around to glare at Willis, and found him leaning casually against the door frame, looking in no way as if he felt guilty.

"Willis?" she said. "What's this doing in here?"

He pushed himself away from the door and casually strode the half-dozen steps it took to stand before her. "I read it," he told her baldly.

"You what?"

He lifted one shoulder and let it drop, but again there was nothing in the gesture to suggest an apology. "I read it," he repeated.

"After I told you to stay away from my things?"

"I couldn't help it, Rosemary," he told her. "At first I thought it was another children's book you had written, and I'd found the first one so charming and intelligently written, that I wanted to read another one."

A little bubble of delight burst inside her, sending a tingle of pleasure through her. But she still felt wary. "You thought it was charming and intelligent? *You?*"

"I thought it was wonderful," he stated flatly. "Obviously, I'm not up on children's books, but you clearly have a talent and skill, not to mention the knowledge and appreciation for it, that will lead to great things."

She narrowed her eyes at him, weighing the words he'd just

associated with her. *Talent. Skill. Knowledge.* ''You think that? About me?''

He nodded. ''And there's something else I think about you, too.''

She was almost afraid to ask. ''What's that?''

''I think I don't ever want to lose you.''

Her mouth went dry, and her brain went haywire. She couldn't swallow, couldn't speak, couldn't think. Which was just as well, because there was evidently more that Willis wanted to tell her.

''I'm not going to apologize for reading your journal,'' he told her again. ''Even if it wasn't a morally upstanding thing for me to do, I'm glad I did it. Because otherwise, I never would have known how you felt about me when we were in high school. Rosemary, I—''

He reached a hand out to her, but she was paralyzed in place, completely unable to do anything but hear what he was saying and be utterly mortified by it. He took another step toward her and covered her hands with his, as if he were going to try to pry the journal out of her frozen fingers. Somehow she managed the strength to tighten her grasp, to refuse him access to the intimate things she had written, even if he'd already read them. For some reason, she just couldn't open herself up that way again.

But instead of trying to take the journal from her, Willis only met her gaze levelly and smiled. Not the arrogant, I-knew-it-all-along-you-sap kind of smile she might have expected, but one of pure, genuine delight. ''You loved me back then.''

It was a statement of fact, not a question, and without even realizing what she was doing, Rosemary nodded her confession of its truth.

His smile fell some, and his eyes darkened as he asked her, ''Do you love me still?''

This time, he was posing a question, his voice and expression holding none of the certainty they had before. But Rosemary's response was the same—a silent nod in the affirmative.

His breath seemed to leave his lungs in a rush of air, and

he crumpled forward, covering her shoulders with his hands, tipping his forehead to hers. "You really love me?" he asked again. "Now?"

"Yes," she managed to whisper. "Pretty stupid of me, huh?"

He shook his head slowly, but didn't pull back from her. "You're not the one who's been stupid, Rosemary," he assured her quietly. "*I'm* the one who's been stupid."

"You?" she asked, incredulous at hearing the admission, yet warmed by it in a way she had never known she could feel. "But you've always been the smartest guy in town," she added, cautioning herself not to feel hopeful, tamping down the happiness she felt blooming deep inside.

The hands on her shoulders slid down to her back, and then Willis pulled her close, hugging her fiercely to himself, as if he feared she would try to push him away. "Not about this," he said. "How a man with such superior intelligence could be such an idiot, I'll never be able to explain. But I have been an idiot, Rosemary."

"Why?"

"Because I never let myself see past your beautiful outside to your beautiful inside, that's why. Because I was completely blind to how talented and intelligent you are. Because I was so busy back in high school trying to keep you from finding out how desperately in love I was with you that I never realized your feelings for me." He pulled back just enough to gaze down into her eyes. "Because I was too stupid to see that you loved me."

She said nothing, waited to see if he would say anything more. The bottom had dropped out of her stomach when he'd admitted that he'd been in love with her in high school, but she couldn't quite let herself believe he still felt that way about her. It was all well and good to have Willis finally realizing that she wasn't a simpleminded, slack-brained know-nothing. It was another matter entirely to see if he still loved her.

"But you know something, Rosemary?" he added, drawing her close again, resting his chin atop her head. "Even though I may be a little slow on the uptake, once I grasp a concept,

I run with it. And one concept I've finally figured out this week, even if Bobrzynyckolonycki does continue to elude me, is that I love you. I always have. And I always will."

"Oh, Willis…"

"And I've been thinking that maybe it might be a good idea to try joining our minds—not to mention a few other body parts—together. Forever. What do you say?"

"Oh, Willis…"

Hot tears sprang into her eyes when she realized what he was asking. What he had told her. What he wanted from her. But all she could say was, "Oh, Willis…"

"Just you and me and those two pesky felines, Isosceles and Scalene. Come on. What do you say?"

She glanced up at him with a smile. "Scalene?"

He nodded. "I don't know if you've ever noticed it, Rosemary, but your cat has a distinctly angular look when she sleeps in that odd way of hers."

She chuckled, blinking back happy tears. "I always thought she looked more like a lopsided ham."

He shook his head. "Scalene triangle. Trust me. So what do you say?" he asked again. "Just the four of us. We'd make a great family."

She forced a little smile, wondering how he was going to react to her next bit of news. "Just the four of us?" she repeated. "What if we have a fifth? If you'll recall, you and I didn't, um…"

"What?"

"We didn't, ah…use anything the other night. If you know what I mean."

She watched as the color drained from his face, then rushed back into his cheeks. Then she heard him chuckle, felt the easy thunder of his laughter rumble up from his chest beneath her fingertips. When she tilted her head back to gaze upon his face, he was smiling at her, in a way she'd never seen him smile before. Happily. Affectionately. Because of her. Because he loved her. Because the thought of having a baby with her brought him joy.

"I think adding to the family is a very good idea, as long as we don't try to name him or her Equilateral."

"Oh, Willis…"

He laughed softly again, then lowered his head to hers, covering her mouth with a warm, wanton kiss. She kissed him back with all the yearning, all the need, all the love that had lain unanswered inside her for half her life, threading her fingers through his hair, cupping his nape with her palm, urging his head down to hers, never wanting to let him go. For some reason, she was suddenly reminded of the wish she'd made fifteen years ago, when Bob had come around the first time. And she smiled against the touch of his mouth on hers.

"What's so funny?" he asked when she, too, chuckled softly.

"I was just remembering something that happened the last time Bob came around."

Willis draped his arms possessively around her waist and bent his head to her neck, nuzzling the soft, fragrant skin he found there. "What?" he asked a little breathlessly.

"You've heard about the myth of the wishes, right?"

He nodded, rubbing his mouth against the slender column of her throat as he did so, smiling when she sucked in a ragged breath and tightened her fingers in his hair. "Mmm…" he said by way of a response. "But I never paid attention to it, having been born two years after Bobrzynyckolonycki came around last time."

"I was born in that year of the comet," she whispered against his temple.

He ran the tip of his tongue along her collarbone and reached for the opening of her blouse. "That's right. I keep forgetting you're an older woman," he said softly as he freed the first button.

She laughed again and dipped her head to taste the inner shell of his ear as he went after the second. "I made a wish the last time Bob came around," she murmured. "The night he made his closest pass to the earth."

Willis freed the third button, lowering his head more as he

did so. "Oh?" he said as he placed a soft kiss on the top of one breast and went to work on her fourth button.

"Oh," she echoed at the intimate touch of his mouth against her. "Oh, yeah."

"What did you wish for?"

"Mmm…I wished that, ooo…my pizza-faced little twerp lab partner, Willis Random, oh…would get what was coming to him someday."

He paused in his actions, then drew back from her, gazing down into her face with an expression she couldn't quite interpret. "You did?"

She nodded, then covered the hand he had halted at her fifth button and helped him unfasten the binding. "Uh-huh."

He smiled as he dropped his hand to the final button and unfastened it, too. Then he scooted his hand beneath her open shirt and covered her breast with sure fingers. She uttered a little sound of sweet surrender when he touched her, then smiled a seductive little smile.

"Why, Rosemary," Willis murmured as he closed his fingers more tightly over her. "How very generous of you to think of me in your wish."

"Mmm," she replied as he found the pebbled peak of her breast and rolled it gently between thumb and forefinger through the lace. "And how very generous of Bob to make that wish come true. For both of us."

"It's the least he can do," Willis said as he lowered his head to the prize his fingers had claimed.

And then there was no time for talk, because he was far too caught up in making wishes come true for both of them. He'd wondered what Rosemary wore beneath her work uniform, he recalled, and now he knew. White wispy scraps of nothing that seemed to melt in his hands and mouth. He covered her nipple through the lace of her brassiere, feeling the hard nub tighten and rise, blossoming under his tongue. Rosemary curled her fingers more tightly in his hair and held him there, whispering words of love, of passion, of promise.

As he tasted her, he tugged her shirttail free of her skirt, then pushed the fabric from her shoulders. A deft finger at the back closure of her bra made haste of that thin barrier, and then he filled his hands and his mouth with the warmth of her bare flesh, touching her softness, tasting her sweetness, drawing her as deeply as he could. In some vague, delirious part of his brain, he sensed her unzipping her skirt, pushing it down over her hips and stepping out of it, and he dropped a hand to the lacy line of her panties.

Reluctantly, he moved his attention away from her breast, dragging soft, quick kisses along her torso, cupping the twin curves of her bottom with firm fingers as he urged her pelvis toward his mouth. Just as he had only moments before, he tasted her again through the damp fabric of her panties, darting his tongue against her hot feminine core until her legs buckled beneath her. Then he scooped her into his arms and laid her carefully on the bed, her back against the mattress, her legs over the side.

Her dark eyes were soft and dewy as she watched him reach behind himself to grab a handful of his shirt and yank it over his head, then deftly unfasten his khaki shorts and strip them off over his legs. His briefs followed, until he stood before her naked, but not once did he feel self-conscious or lacking in any way. The woman waiting for him loved him, and nothing else mattered but that. He moved back toward the bed, but instead of joining her upon it, he knelt on the floor before her.

The musky female scent of her beckoned to him, and he curled the fingers of both hands into the waistband of her panties, then tugged the garment slowly down. He rose and kissed her flat belly, dipped his tongue into the delectable valley of her navel, then lower, where he resumed the feast he had begun only moments before. As he settled his palms firmly over her thighs, Rosemary groaned her surrender, and he smiled as he ducked his head to taste her.

Never before had he wanted a woman the way he wanted her. The desire, the need for her, had plagued him for more than half his life, and he doubted he would ever have his fill of her. So he drank thirstily of her, savored her, consumed her. And when it seemed she would climb to the heights of ecstasy without him, he rose to stand beside the bed, opened her more and drove himself inside her.

Swiftly, smoothly, deeply, irretrievably. Even after he withdrew, a part of him was still inside her. So he plunged himself into her again, deeper still this time, and slowly began to lose himself in a rhythm as old as time.

With each heavy thrust, their bodies moved farther back on the bed, until Willis was kneeling on the mattress before Rosemary, his fingers circling her ankles, taking all of her that she would allow. And as their passion built, he released her and reached for her again, tugging her up toward him, until their slick bodies met from shoulder to thigh. She wrapped her legs around his waist, roped her arms around his neck, covered his mouth with hers and rode him hard.

Willis, too, held on tight to her, unfamiliar with the sensations spiraling through him, almost frightened of what the two of them generated together. Then something inside him burst free, and he wasn't frightened at all. A wild rush of heat and energy and love crashed through him, spilled out of him and into Rosemary, and he knew then that the two of them would be together forever.

Whether what brought them together was a comet, or a wish, or love, or something else that neither of them would ever fully understand, he supposed he would never know. Nor did he care. All that was important was that he and Rosemary were right where they belonged—in each other's arms. Forever.

After they lay spent and exhausted, tangled together in a puzzle of arms and legs and love and contentment, Willis stared out the window at the softly darkening sky. And he thought about Bobrzynyckolonycki. The comet was well on its way out now, speeding through the universe, hurtling toward the sun, taking all its answers with it.

But he knew Bobrzynyckolonycki would be back. In exactly fifteen years.

And next time, Willis, thought, with Rosemary by his side, he'd be ready for the comet. Next time, he'd be waiting for Bobrzynyckolonycki with an even more sophisticated telescope and fifteen more years of learning, study and research. Next time, he'd get that comet pegged, he thought as Rosemary snuggled more intimately against him and sleep overcame him.

Next time, for sure.

*   *   *   *   *

Return to the Towers!

In March
New York Times bestselling author

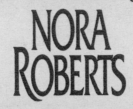

brings us to the Calhouns' fabulous
Maine coast mansion and reveals the
tragic secrets hidden there for generations.

For all his degrees, Professor Max Quartermain has a
lot to learn about love—and luscious Lilah Calhoun is
just the woman to teach him. Ex-cop Holt Bradford is
as prickly as a thornbush—until Suzanna Calhoun's
special touch makes love blossom in his heart.
And all of them are caught in the race to solve
the generations-old mystery of a priceless
lost necklace…and a timeless love.

Lilah and Suzanna
THE
Calhoun Women

**A special 2-in-1 edition containing
FOR THE LOVE OF LILAH and
SUZANNA'S SURRENDER**

Available at your favorite retail outlet.

Take 4 bestselling love stories FREE
Plus get a FREE surprise gift!

ALICIA SCOTT

**Continues the twelve-book series—
36 Hours—in March 1998
with Book Nine**

PARTNERS IN CRIME

The storm was over, and Detective Jack Stryker finally had a prime suspect in Grand Springs' high-profile murder case. But beautiful Josie Reynolds wasn't about to admit to the crime— nor did Jack want her to. He believed in her innocence, and he teamed up with the alluring suspect to prove it. But was he playing it by the book—or merely blinded by love?

For Jack and Josie and *all* the residents of Grand Springs, Colorado, the storm-induced blackout was just the beginning of 36 Hours that changed *everything!* You won't want to miss a single book.

Available at your favorite retail outlet.

COMING NEXT MONTH

#1135 THE SEDUCTION OF FIONA TALLCHIEF—Cait London
The Tallchiefs

Fiona Tallchief was all rebel and raw energy, but she had finally come home to Amen Flats, Wyoming, to settle down. And according to a Tallchief family legend, April's *Man of the Month,* sexy Joel Palladin, was destined to be Fiona's husband. But when Fiona discovered the secret of Joel's parentage, he knew he'd have to carefully seduce this "battlemaiden"… into marriage.

#1136 THE VIRGIN AND THE VAGABOND—Elizabeth Bevarly
Blame It on Bob

Virginal and *still single,* Kirby Connaught launched Operation Mankiller to destroy her nice-girl rep, and perennial playboy James Nash was eager to be her coach. But when local bachelors finally came calling, would James ruin his *own* reputation by committing to only Kirby, forever?

#1137 TAKEN BY A TEXAN—Lass Small
The Keepers of Texas

Socialite Lu Parsons didn't aim to become the best-little-tease-in-Texas when she asked taut-bodied Rip Morris to take care of her, uh, virginity problem. But circumstance kept them at arm's length, simmering and simpering, until Lu risked losing her heart…along with her innocence….

#1138 MATERNITY BRIDE—Maureen Child

One night Denise Torrance dropped all defenses and gave herself over to masterful lover Mike Ryan. And then her unexpected pregnancy set the couple into full swing on the "should-we-shouldn't-we" marriage pendulum. Could baby-on-the-way make these reluctants trust in the longevity of love?

#1139 THE COWBOY AND THE CALENDAR GIRL—Nancy Martin
Opposites Attract

Hank Fowler was no cowboy, but he posed anyway for a hot-hunks-of-the-West calendar contest. When pretty Carly Cortazzo found out her cover guy didn't know a lariat from a love knot would she still be roped into spending forever with a make-believe cowboy?

#1140 TAMING THE TYCOON—Kathryn Taylor

Ultratycoon Ian Bradford held tons of stocks, but lately he'd been focused on *bonds*—the late-night one-on-one kind with voluptuous Shannon Moore. But would their knock-your-socks-off sparks have Ian knocking down hopeful Shannon's door…with a marriage proposal?